The Forgetting Machine

The Flinkwater Chronicles

The Forgetting Machine

Book Two

Pete Hautman

Simon & Schuster Books for Young Readers
New York   London   Toronto   Sydney   New Delhi

SIMON & SCHUSTER BOOKS FOR YOUNG READERS
An imprint of Simon & Schuster Children's Publishing Division
1230 Avenue of the Americas, New York, New York 10020
SIMON & SCHUSTER BOOKS FOR YOUNG READERS is a trademark of Simon &
Schuster, Inc.
For information about special discounts for bulk purchases, please contact Simon &
Schuster Special Sales at 1-866-506-1949 or business@simonandschuster.com.
The Simon & Schuster Speakers Bureau can bring authors to your live event.
For more information or to book an event, contact the Simon & Schuster Speakers
Bureau at 1-866-248-3049 or visit our website at www.simonspeakers.com.
Book design by Chloë Foglia
The text for this book was set in Excelsior LT Std.
Manufactured in the United States of America
0816 FFG
First Edition
10 9 8 7 6 5 4 3 2 1
Library of Congress Cataloging-in-Publication Data
Names: Hautman, Pete, 1952- author.
Title: The forgetting machine / Pete Hautman.
Description: First Edition. | New York : Simon & Schuster Books for Young
Readers, [2016] | Series: The Flinkwater chronicles ; book 2 | Summary:
"Ginger Crump solves the mystery of why people in her town are forgetting
things they should definitely know."—Provided by publisher.
Identifiers: LCCN 2015044664| ISBN 9781481464383 (hardback) |
ISBN 9781481464406 (eBook)
Subjects: | CYAC: Science fiction. | Memory—Fiction. | Mystery and detective stories. |
BISAC: JUVENILE FICTION / Science & Technology. | JUVENILE FICTION / Science
Fiction. | JUVENILE FICTION / Mysteries & Detective Stories.
Classification: LCC PZ7.H2887 Fo 2016 | DDC [Fic]—dc23
LC record available at https://lccn.loc.gov/2015044664

May you never forget what is worth remembering, nor ever remember what is best forgotten.

—an Irish blessing

1

Dead Trees

I found my dad in his study with his nose in a book made out of dead trees. Dad can be embarrassingly retro at times. A *lot* of the times, actually. Like every day. I mean, who reads *paper* books anymore?

Dad has more paper books than he has hairs on his head. Not that he has that many hairs anymore. But still . . . a lot of books. His entire study is lined with the nasty papery things.

He was reading something called *The Island of Dr. Moreau.* I wondered why a doctor would want to live on an island, but I'd learned to never ask my father about *any* book *ever*—a simple polite inquiry was likely to turn into a fifteen-minute lecture.

I took a deep breath and said, "Dad, why is our town called Flinkwater?"

He frowned and shrugged. "Because of the *flink* in the *water*?"

"Dad!"

"Maybe flink is some sort of fish, Ginger. I wouldn't know." One of my father's many quirks is that he hates fish. He won't even eat a tuna sandwich.

"There's no such word as 'flink,'" I said. "I looked it up."

He sighed and closed the book over his index finger to keep his place. If he'd been reading on his tablet, he wouldn't have that problem.

"Why do you ask, Ginger?"

"It's for this stupid school report."

"Maybe the town was founded by somebody named Flinkwater." He shrugged. "I really couldn't say."

"But . . . you're supposed know everything!"

"Apparently I don't," he said.

"Isn't your finger getting squished?"

"A little bit," he said, flipping open the book to ease the pressure.

"How come you don't just read on your tab?"

In my not-so-humble opinion, a proper book should be represented by an icon on a screen. Printing books on paper is as primitive as wearing animal skins or recording music on a plastic disk. Paper books won't let you make the font bigger or smaller, they aren't illuminated, and there's no search function. Also, they take up a lot of space, and they are heavy, unsanitary, unsightly, and noisy—the sound of someone flipping through those dry, whispery pages sets my teeth on edge.

"Studies have shown that reading paper books results in greater memory retention," he said.

"*I* don't have any problem remembering," I said.

"Well, I certainly do. I didn't grow up with e-books. When I was your age, we were still reading on stone tablets."

"Dad!"

He laughed. "Okay, we did have e-books, but they were pretty primitive. Anyway, I'm not taking any chances, what with all the forgetting going on these days."

"All what forgetting?" I asked.

"Several of our people at ACPOD have been experiencing abnormal memory loss," he said. "It's become an epidemic. Just yesterday one of our engineers asked me my name, and he's been working with me for the past ten years."

ACPOD, in case you've been living under a rock for your entire life, is the world's largest manufacturer of Articulated Computerized Peripheral Devices. If you own a robot, it probably came from Flinkwater, Iowa. My parents—along with half the adult population of Flinkwater—work at ACPOD.

"Fortunately, one of our neuroprosthetics experts, Ernie Rausch, has developed an experimental memorization technique that is quite remarkable. He gave me a demonstration, and I now know all fourteen hundred lines of Longfellow's poem 'Evangeline.'"

"That's a lot of lines," I said. "How did you do it?"

"The funny thing is, I don't remember! One minute I was in the neuroprosthetics lab, and the next thing I knew I was back at my desk with my head full of Longfellow. And I couldn't remember my ACPOD password."

"It's Mom's maiden name backward, plus the first seven digits of pi," I said.

He gave me a sharp look. "How do you know that?"

I pointed at the sticky note on the corner of his computer display, where he had written *KNUF3.141592*—not exactly the best way to keep your secret password secret.

"Oh yeah," he said. "Like I said, my memory has been playing tricks on me."

"And you think reading books printed on pulverized wood pulp is the answer?"

"I guess I just prefer *real* books," he said.

I like books too. But I read them on my tablet. Like a normal person.

"Think of all the trees they had to cut down to make the paper," I said.

"Yes, but how many *prehistoric* trees do you think it took to make the crude oil used to make the plastic case for your tablet?"

"Oil doesn't come from trees," I said. "It comes from hundred-million-year-old algae."

He laughed. "Apparently that 'stupid school' is teaching you something. As for the origin of Flinkwater, your mother has lived here her whole life. Ask her."

Before I go on—and I *can* go on—I should introduce myself.

Presenting the fabulous Guinevere Crump—recently turned fourteen, speller of difficult words, defender of helpless animals, fiancée of the smartest boy in the universe, problem solver extraordinaire, revolutionary rabble-rouser, social-justice crusader, and ravishing red-haired beauty—at your service. You may call me Ginger, or on formal occasions, Your Majesty.

So there. I'm glad we got that out of the way.

"Ask your father," said my mother.

"He told me to ask *you*! Your family has been here forever, right? You can't answer a simple question?"

She shot me her glittery, narrow-eyed witch queen look. "Ginger, if it's so simple, why do you ask?"

My mother doesn't scare me. Usually. But she tries.

"It's for school."

"Look it up."

"I tried," I said. Which wasn't completely true. Actually, I'd thought it would be easier to just ask. My mistake. "Do you even *know*?"

"Of course I *know*. I've lived here my entire life. But I'm sure you can figure it out on your own."

"I'm trying to figure it out by asking you."

"Ginger, I'm not going to do your homework for you. I'm busy." She went back to her oh-so-important task: trying to reprogram our DustBot swarm by stabbing at the DustBot control module with her red-nailed fingers. She didn't think the bots were doing a good enough job sucking Barney's cat hair off the carpet. It's Barney's fault. He keeps flipping the bots onto their backs, leaving them to buzz and spin around until somebody turns them right side up.

She might have better luck reprogramming the cat.

"If I get an F, it'll be your fault," I said.

She lowered the control module and gave me a look that was supposed to freeze the blood in my veins. I countered with my wide-eyed-innocent look. It was a mother-daughter standoff.

"Ask your school librarian," she said after a moment.

"Mom, it's Saturday. No school. And next week we get off Monday and Tuesday for teachers' conferences. And my report is due Wednesday."

She arched one precisely plucked eyebrow. "Then you'll just have to go to Flinkwater Memorial."

I was afraid she'd say that.

2

The Stacks

Being the headquarters of ACPOD, Flinkwater is home to a large number of robots. We have more robots than we do humans. Many of the bots, of course, are the little DustBots that keep our houses clean. There are also lawn bots, messenger bots, information bots, and dozens of other specialized robots. But most of Flinkwater's bots work at ACPOD, where they are used to make even more robots.

Flinkwater Memorial Library is one of the few places in town that has no robots whatsoever. I would be forced to deal with a live human being—in this case, the Pformidable Pfleuger.

Ms. Olivia Pfleuger rules the library from behind a wooden counter so high I could rest my chin on it. Both she and the counter have been there since the dawn of time, or possibly before.

From her perch she can see into every corner of the library. Her eyeglasses are as thick as my thumb, but she misses nothing, and she has a memory like an ACPOD server.

As I entered her lair, she peered down at me and said, "Ginger Crump."

She made it sound like an insult. I admit that Crump is not the most elegant and flattering last name in the world, but I'm stuck with it on account of my parents. You might wonder why my mother didn't keep her maiden name when she married my father. It might have to do with the fact that before they got married her name was Amanda *Funk*, which is even worse than Crump.

"I have not forgotten you, Ms. Crump," said the Pformidable Pfleuger.

"I'm sorry," I said.

"Harrumph," she replied.

The Pformidable Pfleuger was referring to the Gum Incident of eight years ago when she caught me sticking a wad of bubble gum to the underside of a chair during a read-aloud event. I was just saving the gum for later, but Ms. Pfleuger didn't see it that way. You'd have thought I'd burned the place down, the way she yelled at me.

I pointed at my open mouth. "Look, no gum."

"Harrumph," she said again.

"I have a question," I said.

"You will find your answer here," she said, waving a thick-fingered hand at the thousands of books lining the walls and stacked on the shelves.

A large sign on the wall above the shelves read COMPUTER-FREE ZONE. Unlike most libraries, Flinkwater Memorial had no computers. It was completely different from the Flinkwater *County* Library in Halibut, which had about forty computer terminals, and no paper books at all. But Flinkwater Memorial, like Ms. Pfleuger herself, was a holdover from the previous millennium—strictly dead trees. Most of the people who went there were old people like my father, people nostalgic for outdated technologies. At the moment there were two men and one woman, all gray-haired and wrinkly, sitting on those uncomfortable wooden library chairs reading furiously.

"I'm not sure where to look," I said.

Ms. Pfleuger compressed her already compressed lips. "What is your question?"

"How come Flinkwater is called Flinkwater?"

I could barely make out her eyes behind those thick glasses, but I was pretty sure they narrowed slightly.

"I would imagine it has to do with the *flink* in the *water*," she said. "Why do you ask?"

"I'm doing a report for school. And there's no such word as 'flink.'"

"I see," she said.

I thought I saw the hint of a smile, but I must have been mistaken. Ms. Pfleuger elevated herself from her chair and descended from her podium. She was a large woman in every dimension other than height, but she moved like a dancer, every step precise. I felt scrawny and awkward next to her.

"Come with me to the stacks," she said.

"Stacks?" I followed her around the desk into a musty-smelling back room I hadn't even known existed. The "stacks" turned out to be where she kept all the old books that nobody wanted to look at: books of all shapes and sizes, presumably organized according to some arcane librarian logic.

I began to sneeze. I'm kind of allergic. Old books are the worst.

"I believe the information you seek may be in Wilhelm Krause's *A History of Flinkwater, Iowa*. Now, let me see if I can find it. . . ." While Ms. Pfleuger perused the crowded shelves, I noticed what appeared to be a stuffed gray cat sitting on the large central table in front of an open book. I had seen stuffed deer heads and so forth, but never an entire stuffed cat. I was wondering why somebody would do that when the cat licked its right paw and turned the page.

"Ms. Pfleuger?" I said, my voice coming out all creaky and weird. "Do you know you have a live cat in your library?"

"Oh, that's just Mr. Peebles."

"Did you know your cat is reading a book?"

Mr. Peebles looked at me, emitted a perfunctory *merp*, and went back to his reading.

"Mr. Peebles is only pretending to read, and he is not my cat. He visits from time to time. I don't mind—he is much better behaved than some of my patrons. Ah, here it is!" She pulled an oversize, frighteningly thick volume from the bottom shelf and handed it to me. I almost dropped it—it must have weighed ten pounds.

"This is volume one. If you can't find the answer to your question there, we also have volumes two and three."

"Can't you just *tell* me?" I said. "I'm kind of in a hurry."

"Please refrain from sneezing on the books," she said, then left me to the mercy of the stacks.

I looked at Mr. Peebles. Mr. Peebles looked at me.

"Stupid cat," I said.

Mr. Peebles hissed.

I sneezed.

3

The Tisks

Wilhelm Krause's *A History of Flinkwater, Iowa* was twelve hundred pages of small, single-spaced font with very few pictures, no index, and no search function. The first two chapters were about the geology of central Iowa. The next three chapters chronicled the various native tribes that had inhabited the area before the arrival of Europeans. The next six chapters were about the Krause family history back in Germany. Needless to say, I flipped through the first half of the book as quickly as I could turn the pages. Except for the title page, the word "Flinkwater" did not appear until chapter 12, which began:

The town of Flinkwater was founded by Gunter Krause in the year 1887 on the banks of the Raccoona River. . . .

The chapter went on to list the names of Gunter Krause's wife and twelve children, followed by a lengthy description of their original homestead, which included all of what was now downtown Flinkwater. The book mentioned some of the other early settlers: the Johnsons, the Grossmans, and the Funks. I was surprised by that last one. I knew my mom's family had lived in Flinkwater for several generations, but I didn't know they had lived here before the town was even a town.

I skimmed through the rest of the book but could find no clues as to why Gunter Krause had named the town Flinkwater. By the time I got to the end, the only thing keeping me from slipping into a coma was my sneezing.

"This is ridiculous," I said to Mr. Peebles.

"Merp."

"I agree." I closed the book and returned it to its place, more or less—I was sneezing ferociously at the time and may have got it on the wrong shelf. Mr. Peebles followed me back into the main room, where Ms. Pfleuger was being confronted by the infamous Tisks.

Mr. and Mrs. Tisk looked like a set of salt-and-pepper shakers. She, with her fluffy crown of bleach-blond hair, was salt. Mr. Tisk, with a similar bouffant in gray-speckled black, was pepper. They were about the same size and shape, with shiny, hairless faces perched atop rounded shoulders, bodies swelling below to bulbous middles, then tapering down to two smallish pairs of shoes, hers white, his polished black.

Standing behind them, staring at the floor with slumped shoulders, was Dottie Tisk. I hardly recognized her. She was wearing a long dress, almost to her ankles, and a pair of lace-up granny shoes. Her mouse-brown hair was pulled back tight in a short ponytail, and her skin was white as lard.

Back in the sixth grade, Dottie had been the first girl in school to wear makeup. She would slather on lipstick and eyeliner on the way to school, and sometimes pin up her skirt to make it a few inches shorter. Some kids thought she looked glamorous, others considered her kind of trampy. I just thought she was interesting, even though we were never close friends. I remember she was really smart, even by Flinkwater standards.

After school, on her way home, she would wipe off the makeup and lower the hem of her skirt. Her parents must have caught her, because halfway through the year they pulled her out of school, and I never saw her around town after that. I had heard they sent her off to some super-religious boot camp.

Mr. Tisk was the pastor of Glorious Heart Ministries, a hard-core evangelical church located outside of town, just downwind of Elwin Hogg's hog farm. Mr. Tisk's congregation was small but avid, with a tremendous tolerance for hellfire-and-damnation sermons and the smell of pig poop.

"Hey, Dottie," I said.

She gave me a quick look, then returned her eyes to the floor. I got the sense she was embarrassed. Her parents did not acknowledge me at all. Mr. Tisk was glaring at Ms. Pfleuger, who was glaring back at him. Mrs. Tisk was smiling blankly, gripping her purse with both hands.

Mr. Tisk was holding a book in his right hand. He raised it above his head and slammed it down onto the counter.

"This," he proclaimed loudly, "is wicked, sacrilegious filth!"

I looked at the book cover. To my surprise, it was *Charlotte's Web*, a book I had been meaning to read. In fact, I had it loaded up on my tab. If I'd known it was all wicked and sacrilegious I'd have read it sooner.

The Pformidable Pfleuger's glare intensified to a degree that *should* have set his eyebrows on fire, but Mr. Tisk had no eyebrows. Perhaps he had lost them in an earlier encounter.

"Talking *pigs*!" he said. "Talking *rats*! Talking *spiders*!" He thumped the Bible he carried in his other hand. *"There are no talking animals in the Bible!"*

I said, "What about the serpent in the Garden of Eden?"

Mr. Tisk aimed his glare in my direction.

"The voice of Satan!" he said. I wasn't sure if he was talking about me or the serpent.

"I'm just saying," I said.

Mr. Tisk's normally fish-belly-white face flared red. He turned back to Ms. Pfleuger and thumped the cover of *Charlotte's Web* with his finger—"*This* is *not* suitable for children!"

"Fine," said Ms. Pfleuger. "You are free to prevent *your* child from reading whatever you like, but you do not speak for my other patrons."

"*All* children are children of the Lord!"

Just then Dottie noticed Mr. Peebles winding his way around her feet.

"Mr. Peebles!" she exclaimed, scooping him up. "Where have you been?" She hugged the cat to her chest.

"He's been right here, Dottie," said Ms. Pfleuger, "reading books of which your father no doubt disapproves."

"Animals do not read," said Mr. Tisk.

"Mr. Peebles does," I said.

"Tsk!" said Mrs. Tisk.

I've noticed that in books, characters often

say "tsk" or "tsk-tsk." But in real life, nobody says "tsk." Except for Mrs. Tisk, and not just when she is telling people her name.

"Is there anything else I can do for you?" said Ms. Pfleuger. Her tone of voice was more like *Get your book-banning butts out of my library!*

"I will be bringing this up at the next town council meeting," said Mr. Tisk. "We will do whatever is necessary to protect children—*all* children—from this wickedness, and we will not stop until we burn every last copy."

"You can't set fire to an e-book," I blurted.

Mr. Tisk's head swiveled toward me.

"And you would be . . . ?" he said.

"I would be Ginger Crump, and I'm just saying that book burning doesn't work so well when there are millions of digital copies everywhere." I smiled at Ms. Pfleuger, thinking she would approve of my clever rejoinder, but she was scowling at me just as hard as Mr. Tisk.

Mr. Tisk smirked. "Your precious e-books are no match for the forces of righteousness," he said. "I'll see that every last copy of that book, paper or electronic, will be turned to ashes—starting now!"

He lunged for the book, but Ms. Pfleuger was faster—she snatched up *Charlotte's Web* and held it out of his reach.

"You will do no such thing," she said, her voice

shaking with barely suppressed rage. "Now please leave before I am forced to call the police."

Mr. Tisk withdrew his clawed hands. "Very well, then. We shall see. There are many paths to righteousness. Come along, Mrs. Tisk. Come, Dottie. It's time for us to do the Lord's work." Mr. and Mrs. Tisk spun on their heels and marched off. Dottie, still holding Mr. Peebles, turned slowly and followed them out the door.

"Poor Dottie," Ms. Pfleuger said. "She used to come in here all the time, but since her parents began homeschooling her two years ago, I've hardly seen her. She came in last week and checked out *Charlotte's Web*." She sighed. "After this, I expect I won't see her again."

"Dottie's been homeschooled? I thought they sent her away someplace."

"No, she's been here all along, but she isn't allowed to leave the house without her parents."

"No wonder she looks so pasty. At least they let her have a cat."

"Yes, although she isn't very good at keeping him at home. Mr. Peebles has been stopping by quite often lately." She shrugged. "I don't mind. For a cat, he is quite intelligent."

"Well, he *does* live in Flinkwater."

Flinkwater, as I'm sure you know, is home to a large number of very smart people. It's all because of Gilbert Bates, the founder and CEO of ACPOD. Years ago he hired the smartest scientists and engineers he could find and brought them all to Iowa. *Tech Titans* magazine once estimated that the average IQ in Flinkwater is twenty points higher than the national average, which is ridiculous. I'm quite certain it's much higher.

Also, we have at least one very smart cat.

"Did you find out why our town is called Flinkwater?" Ms. Pfleuger asked.

"Not exactly."

"I have several other books you could look into."

"That's okay," I said. There was no way I was going to plow through more sneeze- and sleep-inducing paper history. "I think I'm all booked out for the day." I looked at the copy of *Charlotte's Web* on her desk. "But that story sounds pretty interesting, with a talking spider and all."

"You haven't read *Charlotte's Web*?" Ms. Pfleuger looked horrified. "You must! Would you like to check it out?"

"Um . . . no thanks. I have the e-book on my tab; I just haven't got around to reading it yet."

"*E*-book?" Ms. Pfleuger snorted. "E-books will *never* replace *real* books." She opened the book to a picture of a pig eating from a trough. "What about these beautiful illustrations?"

"I'm pretty sure the e-book has all the pictures," I said.

"Pixels on a screen can never replace ink on paper! This electronica you are so enamored of is untrustworthy and unfaithful! *Printed* books are *solid!*" She thumped *Charlotte's Web* with her forefinger. "Printed books are *real!* E. B. White must be spinning in his grave! Do you think he would want his masterpiece reduced to a flickering collection of bits and bytes?"

"My tab doesn't flicker." I backed away nervously. "And it's not flammable."

"One computer glitch and *poof!*" Ms. Pfleuger flailed her arms in a fit of librarian passion. "All your books disappear!"

"I'm pretty sure I could just download them again," I said.

"One day you'll see, Ginger Crump. Mark my words!"

"Thank you," I said as I backed out the door. I'd always known that the Pformidable Pfleuger was a bit odd, but I hadn't realized until that moment that, in her own way, she was just as crazy as the Tisks.

4

Billy Bates

It was a huge relief to get out of the library, but I still had my Flinkwater problem to deal with. Clearly, it was time to employ my secret weapon.

Billy Bates, whose name used to be Billy George,[1] was the son of Gilbert Bates. That meant that Billy was fabulously wealthy, and he was my fiancé—or at least I planned for him to be. Since Billy and I were only fourteen, our wedding date had not yet been set. Also, he didn't know about it.

Lest you think that I am some sort of gold-digging hussy, my plans to marry Billy were formed long before he got rich.[2] I fell in love with him for his other qualities: great hair, cute smile, kissable lips, and an amazing brain. In fact, Billy was the smartest person on the planet.

---

1 You can read about why in our earlier adventure, *The Flinkwater Factor*.
2 That story is also told in *The Flinkwater Factor*.

Or at least the smartest one I have ever met. Which was why I headed straight from the library to his house.

Billy and his dad lived in the biggest house in Flinkwater, built seventy years ago by wealthy corn baron Wilhelm Krause—the same Wilhelm Krause who had written the snooze-worthy *History of Flinkwater, Iowa*. The house was pretty cool. It had about twenty rooms, and turrets on the corners, and a tall iron fence with all sorts of curlicues and spikes that were supposed to represent corn tassels but looked more like deadly weapons.

I pushed through the iron gate, followed the cobblestone walk up to the front door, and rang the bell. Alfred, their new butler, let me in.

"Ms. Crump. How lovely to see you again!"

Alfred was an imposing fellow, but always polite. He was probably the only butler in all of Flinkwater. And he was most certainly the only one with a single multifaceted omnidirectional eye, two retractable pneumatic arms, and three rubber-clad motilators instead of feet. Including his sensor array, Alfred stood slightly more than six feet tall.

As you may have guessed, Alfred was a robot.

"Thank you, Alfred. You are looking quite handsome today."

"I find you handsome as well, Ms. Crump."

"I'm not handsome," I said. "I'm ravishing."

"Would you care for a grilled cheese sandwich?" he said.

"I'm not *ravenous*, Alfred. I'm *ravishing*!"

He stood without moving or making a sound
for a few seconds, then said, "Communication error
alert. Please rephrase."

"Never mind. Is Billy home?"

"Yes."

"Will you tell him I'm here, please?"

"I have already notified Master Billy. This
way, please." Alfred rotated on his motilators and
headed off down the hall. I followed. We had gone
only a few feet when one of Alfred's hydraulic arms
shot out to the side and punched a hole in the wall.

He retracted his arm and kept moving. I
stopped.

"Er . . . Alfred?"

Alfred halted. His sensor array rotated to
face me.

"Yes, Ms. Crump?"

"Why did you punch a hole in the wall?"

"Invasive species control function," he said.

I examined the damage to the wall—a perfect
circle half an inch deep. In the center of the depres-
sion was what appeared to be a flattened insect.

"You killed a fly," I said, "but you also made a
hole in the wall."

Alfred took a moment to consider that.

"Recalibration in progress," he said. "This way, please."

As we continued along the hall, I noticed a few other spots where plaster had crumbled and flies had died. I made a mental note to avoid getting between Alfred and any invasive species.

When we reached the stairwell, Alfred opened the door and stood aside.

"Thank you, Alfred." I headed down the stairs to Billy Bates's lair. If I lived there, I would want one of the round rooms in the turrets, but Billy had claimed an old subbasement bomb shelter as his domain. As expected, he was sitting in his swivel chair facing a bank of high-definition screens. Four games were running. I recognized Black Ops XIV, Ghast Wars, and Interzone Apocalypse. The fourth display showed shadowy figures moving in and out of a nearly black image space, with occasional splashes of red. Blood, I assumed.

"What's that?" I asked, pointing.

"New MOG," he said.

MOG, in case you don't know, stands for multiplayer online game. Billy was the only person I knew who could play three or four of them at once.

"It's called Deathdark."

"Very catchy," I had to admit.

"I hacked into their servers—you know, just to try it out. It's a pre-beta release."

"Speaking of pre-beta—did you know that your butler is punching holes in your walls?"

Billy turned to look at me, flipping his thick dark hair off his forehead. Have I mentioned his hair? Have I mentioned his molten-brown eyes to die for?

"He's still doing that?" he said.

"You knew? And you let him answer the door? What if a fly had landed on my forehead?"

"Good point. I'll mention it to Gilly." Gilly was Billy's father, better known as Gilbert Bates. Most people called him Mr. Bates, but Billy and I called him Gilly, because we were friends with him before we found out he was actually Billy's father.[3]

"I have a problem," I said. "I need to find out why Flinkwater is called Flinkwater."

"Because of all the *flink* in the *water*?"

"Why do people keep *saying* that?"

"It's the obvious inference," Billy said.

"Well it's wrong! Come on, Billy. I have a report due for history class on Wednesday, and I need help. Can't you use your Web magic?"

Billy sighed and switched off his game screens. "Okay, but I have school problems of my own, you know."

"You?"

"Me."

---

3 Yes, yes, you can read about that in *The Flinkwater Factor* too. And I promise this will be the last irritating footnote!

"Tell me! Maybe I can help!"

Billy gave me a look I can only describe as nervous, or perhaps fearful. I may have come across as a little too eager. Also, the last time I'd tried to help Billy with a problem, we'd both ended up in jail.[4]

"Seriously," I said. "What's the problem?"

"I failed a couple tests, so Gilly hired a tutor."

"Oh." A tutor! *That* was embarrassing. Especially for a kid so smart he'd skipped three grades. "How come you failed?"

"I got bored. One was an American history test, multiple choice. I chose *B* for the whole test. And then I had to write this essay for language arts and I did it in pig latin. Mr. McPhee said *ix-nay* on *at-thay*." He shrugged. "I was just messing around."

"Can't you just explain to your dad?"

"Gilly's off on one of his work binges. He's practically living at ACPOD. Last time he came home, I'm not sure he even recognized me—you know how he gets."

I did know. Gilbert Bates was the smartest person I'd ever met, next to Billy, but he could be quite absentminded.

"Yeah, my dad's been a little spacey too," I said. "What's he working on?"

"It's top secret."

---

4   Okay, I lied about no more footnotes. But this is it, I swear.

"*Everything* at ACPOD is top secret, but that never stopped you from unsecreting it."

"True," Billy said, "but you have to promise not to tell anybody. It's a drone."

"What's so hush-hush about a drone?" I asked.

Drones, of course, have been around a long time. Chances are the last time you ordered a pizza, it was delivered by drone. In fact, Pizza Hut has more drones than the US military.

"It's not just any drone," Billy said. "Most drones have propellers, like helicopters. This new drone is powered by antigravity waves. No propellers, just a disk about three feet across. Completely silent. It can carry up to a hundred pounds."

"So you could ride around on it? Like a magic carpet?"

Billy looked down at his slightly rounded belly. "Maybe *you* could."

"Maybe the next prototype will carry more weight. How come it's so secret?"

"Gilly doesn't want to take any chances that the antigravity tech will be leaked until he can figure out a way to control it. He's been working on the project solo—that's why he's been working so much."

Bing!

"What was that?" I asked.

"Alfred is telling me that Mr. Rausch is here."

"Who?"

"The tutor."

"Oh. Maybe you'll get lucky."

Billy cocked his head. "How so?"

"Maybe a bug will land on his chin, and Alfred will do his thing."

5

The Tutor

Mr. Rausch, a tall, whippet-lean, long-limbed man, ducked through the door to Billy's room and looked around with a sour expression. His narrow, tightly compressed lips were framed by a neatly trimmed mustache and a goatee that jutted from his chin like a black spike. His hair was slicked back and held in place by some sort of shiny substance. He was wearing black jeans and a white dress shirt fastened at the neck with a bolo tie. A sweet, spicy odor, like cloves steeped in rubbing alcohol, wafted off him.

A smallish white bulldog of opposite proportions waddled in after him.

"I am Ernest Rausch," he said. "You may call me Mr. Rausch." He gestured at the dog. "This is Gertrude. She is a French bulldog."

Gertrude rolled her eyes and drooled.

"What is that smell?" I asked. I know it was rude of me, but sometimes the words just pop out.

Mr. Rausch gave his dog a reproving look. "Gertrude! Shame on you!"

"Not the dog," I said. "It's more like a cleaning product. Kind of clovey."

Mr. Rausch drew back. "Are you referring to my Bay Rum?" he asked.

"It does smell sort of rummy," I said.

"Bay Rum is a classic men's aftershave. Discriminating people find it pleasing." He examined me critically. "Are you Billy Bates?"

"Do I look like a *boy* to you?" I said, horrified. Clearly, Mr. Rausch and I were not destined to get along.

He pursed his lips and narrowed his eyes. "Despite your unflattering jeans and T-shirt, you appear to be a rather thin girl with extraordinarily curly, somewhat reddish hair and a large number of freckles, but I try not to make assumptions based upon physical appearance. Furthermore, the name Billy is not necessarily gender specific. Billie Holiday, for example, was a woman."

"I'm *Ginger*, and I'm a *girl*." I pointed at Billy. "*He's* Billy."

He turned his eyes to Billy.

"I understand you are having trouble with American history and language arts."

"I was having a bad day," Billy said.

"With my REMEMBER learning system, we can make sure you don't have any more bad days."

"Remember system?" Billy said.

"REMEMBER. It is an acronym for the Really Excellent Memory Enhancement Method by Ernest Rausch. It can enable you to memorize pi to ten thousand digits."

"Cool!" Billy said.

"Wouldn't that take up a lot of room in your brain?" I asked.

They both looked at me.

Mr. Rausch said, "And you are . . . ?"

"Ginger? Girl? Rather *thin*? Who you just met, like, sixty seconds ago?"

"Correct!" said the tutor, as if I'd just responded to a test question. "As for memories taking up physical space, that is not a problem. Even Gertrude, for example, has the capacity to remember tens of thousands of smells, sounds, and images, and her brain is less than half the size of yours."

Gertrude looked up at the sound of her name and snorfled.

"She just radiates intelligence," I said.

"She knows more than you can imagine," Mr. Rausch said.

"I can imagine a lot," I said.

He sniffed and returned his attention to Billy.

"I thought we could start with history. Have you memorized the Declaration of Independence and the United States Constitution and its amendments?"

"Er ... not exactly," Billy said. "Isn't that like a hundred pages?"

"Not precisely."

"I don't think that's something we have to do for school," I said.

"My method requires a solid foundation in the basics," he said. "Furthermore, it works best when my tutee and I are able to work without constant interruptions. In other words ... "

"I was just leaving," I said.

So much for Billy being my secret weapon. The mystery of Flinkwater would have to wait until he was done getting tutored, or REMEMBERed, or whatever. I was a bit peeved at him, to tell the truth.

After what happened to him later, I felt pretty bad about that.

On the way home I was trying to figure out how to write my paper for Mr. Westerburg's class without subjecting myself to further mortification or library sneeze-fests, when I noticed I was being followed.

I'd been followed before, like a couple months ago when the Department of Homeland Security thought I was a terrorist.[5] Their black SUVs are easy to spot, but they hadn't been bothering me lately.

But this was no black SUV following me. This was a familiar-looking gray cat.

"Mr. Peebles, is there something I can do for you?" I asked politely.

Mr. Peebles stopped walking, sat down on the sidewalk, and looked off at something utterly fascinating to him but completely invisible to me. The way one does, if one is a cat.

I continued toward home. Mr. Peebles let me get about twenty feet away, then continued to follow me. He followed me all the way to my front door, where I stopped to explain the situation to him.

"Mr. Peebles, inside this house there is a Siamese cat. His name is Barney, and he is a jealous cat who believes that all other cats are evil demons. You should go home."

"Merp?" said Mr. Peebles, tilting his head.

"Yes, merp," I said. "Now go home."

If that cat understood what I was saying, he chose to ignore it.

"Scat!" I yelled, waving my arms vigorously.

Mr. Peebles backed up to the spirea bush and left his stinky calling card. He then trotted over by the maple tree, tucked his feet beneath his body, and closed his eyes to slits.

---

5   Oops. I said I wasn't gonna do this.

6

DustBots

My mother had made significant progress with the DustBots, if causing them all to clump up in the corner of the living room could be called progress. When I walked in, she was stabbing commands into the handheld control module while yelling at the bots to disperse. My mother is not a woman who is accustomed to being ignored. But the DustBots didn't seem to know that.

Just in case you have been marooned on a tropical island for the past two decades, I should explain about DustBots.

Imagine a gerbil. Bigger than a mouse, smaller than a rat, and cuter than either. Now imagine that instead of fur it has a shiny plastic case in your choice of eight colors, and instead of being alive it is a robot. Now imagine your home, only very, very clean. When activated, an ACPOD

DustBot will seek out dirt, dust, and other undesirable substances and transport them to the kitchen trash can.

The DustBot was invented by Gilbert Bates seventeen years ago. It is the single most successful tech product in history—the average home in the United States has three DustBots. The average home in Flinkwater has nine. We have seventeen, and all of them were huddled in one corner of the living room, humming and buzzing.

This was not normal DustBot behavior.

Barney was crouched a few feet away, keeping an eye on them.

"Mom, what did you do to the bots?"

"I have no idea." She thrust the control mod at me. "See if you can fix it."

I checked the display on the mod and saw right away that she had accidentally activated the herding function. I turned it off. The pile of bots began to disperse, their randomizers sending them off in every direction, searching for dirt.

Barney sprang into action. Before I could stop him, he flipped three of them onto their backs. I scooped him up and turned the bots right side up.

"I was hoping to program them to avoid the cat," Mom said.

"Barney does not choose to be avoided," I said. "By the way, I went to the library. I looked through everything they had on Flinkwater"—a slight exaggeration—"and found nothing. So I'll probably fail history."

"That is unfortunate," she said, and from the set of her jaw, I saw that she would be no help, despite that fact that I had just helped *her* with the DustBots.

I went to tell Dad that Mom was going to let me flunk Mr. Westerburg's class. I found him standing in the hallway staring down at Barney.

"What is this creature doing in our house?" he asked.

"That's Barney," I said. "He's a cat," I added sarcastically.

"Who is Barney?" he asked.

"*That* is Barney," I said. "Our *cat?*"

"We have a cat?"

"Dad!" I hated when he teased me.

"When did we get a cat?"

"Eight years ago!"

The look he gave me was one of utter confusion. He really didn't remember. Like most older people, Dad can be absentminded at times. I mean, he's in his forties. But not remembering Barney?

"Dad, are you okay?"

"Certainly," he said, but he still had that puzzled look on his face. "How could I forget old Blarney?"

"Not *Blarney*! Barney!" I was getting more worried by the second.

"Yes, of course. Er . . . is there something I can help you with?"

"Not unless you've remembered how Flinkwater got its name."

"Sorry. My memory's not what it used to be, Ginger."

At least he remembered *my* name.

7

Mr. Peebles

Mom was at the bathroom sink using a tint comb to touch up the roots of her spiky black hair. She is serious about her hair and her nails. Every hair must be raven black from tip to root, and every nail must be red, sharp, and gleaming. It's part of her patented witch-queen look. She likes to be intimidating. She says it comes in handy at work.

"Mom, Dad forgot we have a cat."

"I wish I could."

"It's not funny. He just asked me who Barney was."

"I'm sure he was just distracted—as I am at this moment."

"He told me this morning that there's an epidemic of forgetfulness at ACPOD. Maybe he caught something."

"I'm sure he didn't mean 'epidemic' literally, Ginger."

"Yeah but what if he did?"

"It's not all bad. There are several things I would not mind forgetting. How do I look?" She leaned her head toward me. "Any gray showing?"

"There wasn't any before you started, Mom."

"Good. That's when you want to catch it."

A horrific screeching came from downstairs.

My mother looked at me and said, "I understand we have a cat."

I ran downstairs and followed the caterwauling. All the yowling was coming from Barney, who was standing stiff-legged on top of the refrigerator looking down at Mr. Peebles, who had somehow gotten into the house and onto the kitchen counter. Several of the cupboard doors were standing open. Mr. Peebles was digging into the one we used for canned stuff, sorting through it with his paws, pushing aside the baked beans, stewed tomatoes, and various soups.

"Mr. Peebles!" I said. "How did you get in here?"

He looked at me over his shoulder and said, "Merp."

Barney hissed.

"What are you doing?" I asked.

Mr. Peebles reached deep into the cupboard

and clawed out a can of tuna. The can fell to the counter and rolled off the edge onto the floor. He hopped down next to it and looked up at me.

"Mrowr?"

Barney, who also knew his way around a can of tuna, fell silent. Both cats were staring at me with that insistent look—you know the one—where they are trying to eat you with their eyes. Frankly, it was a little spooky.

"Okay," I said. "You win." I opened the can and divided it into two bowls. Both cats were twining around my feet, best of friends now that they had a common mission. I put the bowls down and watched them eat. It took about twenty seconds. After they finished eating, Barney turned his back on Mr. Peebles and proceeded to lick his paws, having decided to pretend that there was no strange cat in the house. Mr. Peebles went to the back door and silently commanded me to open it.

"Hang on a minute," I said. I went to get Barney's cat crate. If I could coax Mr. Peebles into it, I'd take him back to the Tisks, who lived just a few blocks away. Everybody knew where the Tisks lived. It was the only house in town with a life-size, smiling, blond, blue-eyed Jesus statue in the front yard. But before I could get the crate, I heard the screen door slam. I ran back to the kitchen. Mr. Peebles had somehow opened the door and let himself out. I caught a glimpse of him as he disappeared over the backyard fence.

I looked at Barney. Barney looked at me.

"I'm glad you're not that smart," I said.

He lashed his tail and strutted off in search of a DustBot.

Charlotte, the spider in the book *Charlotte's Web*, could write and spell better than some of those people.

I wasn't sure about that last bit. I knew Charlotte was a spider who spun words in her web, but I hadn't actually read the book. I wasn't sure about the spelling thing.

Since I'd been meaning to read it anyway, and Mr. Tisk had made it sound so interesting, I pulled up the document on my tab, flopped down on my bed, and dove in. It took all of ten seconds for me to get completely absorbed in the story. I'd read all the way to chapter 11—that's when Charlotte writes her first words—when my mom yelled at me to set the table for dinner.

"Just a minute!" I yelled back, and kept on reading. I was relieved to find that Charlotte the spider could spell just fine. I wouldn't have to change my report.

My mom started yelling again, so I set my tab aside and stomped downstairs.

"I was doing homework," I said.

"Well *I'm* doing *house*work," she said. All she was doing was putting a frozen lasagna in the microwave oven, which barely qualifies as work, and certainly isn't as technically challenging as setting the table. But I had the sense not to point that out. Mom was quite proud of her microwaving skills.

8

Charlotte's Web

I figured if a cat was smart enough to read a book, break into a house, order dinner, and open a door, then *I* was smart enough to figure out how to write my Flinkwater report without wasting more time on unnecessary research. I'd just make something up. I mean, if the origins of the Flinkwater name were so mysterious, Mr. Westerburg probably didn't know either. I sat down at my desk and began to compose my report.

There are many theories as to the origin of the town nam Flinkwater. Some believe that "flink" is a Native Americ word meaning "sweet," or possibly "putrid." Or maybe if the name of a fish. Or possibly Flinkwater is a misspel of Fairview or some other common town name, as ba in the old days people did not have spell-check, and handwriting was practically impossible to read. Ev

I set the table quickly, hoping to get back to my book for another chapter or two before dinner.

It was not to be. As I was setting the table, she rattled off a list of other Important Tasks that required my Immediate Attention.

"You left your shoes on the floor by the front door, the ficus plant needs water, and the cat box needs emptying."

"Mom, I'm not a bot!"

"Neither am I. Now hurry up; dinner will be ready in thirteen minutes."

Glumly I set about my assigned tasks. The cat box was the worst. Barney watched me scoop out his old turds, waiting patiently so that he could start the process all over again.

"You are very stinky," I told him.

"Merp," he agreed.

I wasn't able to get back to *Charlotte's Web* until after dinner, and there was a nasty surprise waiting for me. When I started on chapter 12, I became immediately confused. All the characters had changed:

One evening, a few days after the writing had appeared on the wall, Charlotte called a meeting of all the children in the barn cellar.

"I shall begin by calling the roll. Wilbur?"

"Here!" said the boy.

"George?"

"Here, here, here!" said George.

I stopped reading. Writing on what *wall*? What *children*? Who was *George*? And Wilbur is supposed to be a *pig*, not a *boy*!

It was a completely different book. I flipped back to the previous chapter. Everything had changed. All the animals had been replaced by kids, and instead of a spider writing words in her web, it was a girl named Charlotte writing on a wall. It made no sense at all!

Something—or someone—had hacked into my copy of *Charlotte's Web* and changed all the words.

9

A Tisk Problem

I took my tablet to ACPOD's director of cyber-security services, who just so happens to be my father.

"This *is* rather odd," he said, looking at the corrupted text on my tab.

"It's more than odd," I said. "It's literary terrorism."

"I wouldn't go quite that far. Have you tried downloading a fresh copy?"

"Yes! It's the same."

"Let me try." He picked up his own tablet and logged on to the county library system. A few seconds later *Charlotte's Web* popped up.

"Hmmm," he said, scrolling through the first few chapters. "Is Charlotte supposed to be a little girl who writes on walls?"

"No!"

"I didn't think so. It seems the library file has been corrupted as well. Let me check out some other titles."

A few minutes later he had looked over the digital editions of *The Island of Dr. Moreau, The Adventures of Huckleberry Finn,* and *War and Peace.*

"These all look fine," he said.

"I know who did this," I said.

Nothing is ever simple.

If I were in charge, I'd have ordered an immediate SWAT raid on the Tisks and hung them up by their thumbs until they agreed to fix *Charlotte's Web.*

That's probably why I'm not in charge.

"Ginger, we don't know with any certainty that Mr. and Mrs. Tisk are behind this," my dad said.

"Who else would replace all the talking animals with talking humans?"

"It could be one of their parishioners, or any number of other people. What we need to do is wait until Monday and contact the administrator at the county library system. They'll be able to restore the damaged texts and trace the invasive bug back to its source."

"But I need Charlotte *now,*" I whined. I am not above whining. Sometimes it works.

"Then you'll have to borrow a paper copy."

"From *who?* The library's closed!"

"Maybe one of your friends?"

"You're the only person I know who reads paper books! Can't you just go over to the Tisks and tell them if they don't fix it they'll be in big trouble? Mom would."

He laughed. I hate it when he laughs while I'm trying to be serious.

"Maybe you should pitch this to her, then."

"Maybe I will!"

"Good luck."

I have to explain about my mother. My mom is scary. I've mentioned her long, blood-red fingernails and her glittery eyes and her crown of spiky black hair, but I haven't told you she is six feet tall with a tongue that could slice a steel bar into frightened little disks. She would be the perfect weapon to unleash upon the Tisks—if I could get her with the program.

That was the problem. Mom is big on self-reliance, as in, *Ginger, do not ask me to solve your Flinkwater problem for you.*

In other words, she is not the nurturing type.

I found her in the backyard enjoying herself in a quiet sort of way by pinching beetles off her rosebush.

"Mom, did you ever read *Charlotte's Web*?"

"The book about the pig and the spider?" she said. "I could use a spider right now. Look at what these creatures are doing to my flowers."

"Yeah, I could use a spider too. But I have a Tisk problem."

"Tisk problem?"

"Yes. Mr. and Mrs. Tisk have hacked my tab." I explained what had happened and how I was sure the Tisks were involved. Several rose beetles met their doom as I spoke.

"Your father is the cyber-security expert. Did you talk to him?"

"He says he'll contact the county library on Monday, but I was hoping maybe you could talk to the Tisks before that."

"And why is this so urgent?"

"I need to finish reading about Charlotte."

"Don't you have other things you could be doing? Have you finished that report you were working on?"

"*Charlotte's Web* is part of my research."

"How is a book about talking animals pertinent to a paper about the history of Flinkwater?"

"It's complicated," I said.

"I'm sure it is," she said as she pinched the head off another beetle.

It was no great surprise that my mother the beetle pincher had refused my desperate call for help. As I said before, she was not the nurturing type. Clearly, I would have to take matters into my own hands.

10

Ransom Note

The life-size Jesus statue in the Tisks' front yard made an excellent guardian. His blue eyes seemed to follow me as I walked past him, silently reminding me of all ten commandments and how I'd broken at least four of them. I didn't think I was breaking any at the moment, but he still made me kind of nervous. I rang the doorbell. A few seconds later the door opened and Mrs. Tisk was staring out at me. Or maybe she was looking *through* me—it was hard to tell. She reminded me of the statue, only less alive. She didn't say anything; she just stood there with her crown of pale blond hair and colorless eyes.

"Hi, Mrs. Tisk," I said. "I'm Ginger Crump."

"I know who you are." Her voice sounded like oatmeal. "You are the girl from the library. What is it you want?"

I held up my tab and showed her a page from the corrupted version of *Charlotte's Web*.

"Charlotte isn't supposed to be a girl. She's a spider. I want you to fix it, because if you don't, you're going to be in big trouble." When I had practiced saying that on the way over, it had sounded much more fearsome. Mrs. Tisk's dead-fish eyes bored into me. "My dad will have you arrested for literary terrorism," I added.

Mrs. Tisk laughed, a creaky, rusty sound like you might hear if you forced open a cellar door that hadn't been opened in decades.

"You can't just go around changing books," I said.

"Your blasphemous reading habits are not my concern, young lady. Clearly you are not only rude and presumptuous, you are beyond saving. I have no idea what you're talking about, and even if I did, I wouldn't care. However, I will pray for you."

She slammed the door in my face.

But not before her cat, Mr. Peebles, slipped out unseen.

"How do you stand it?" I asked him.

"Grup," he said.

I did not mean to become a kidnapper. Or, more accurately, a *cat*napper. Mr. Peebles followed me home of his own free will. And when we got there, I did not force him to stay, but I did feed him another half a can of tuna. I gave the other half to Barney, making him promise not to say anything. Grudgingly Barney agreed. He ate his tuna and went to his living room perch to sulk. I politely invited Mr. Peebles to spend the night in my bedroom, and he politely accepted my invitation.

Why did I do that? I suppose I was angry that the Tisks had taken Charlotte away from me, and thousands of other readers, and taking their cat was . . . I don't know. I was mad, okay? Anyway, I figured I could return Mr. Peebles later and no harm done. And they couldn't really blame me, because Mr. Peebles had come on his own.

I considered sending a ransom note. I spent a few minutes writing one out. I found a ransom note font to make it look like a real ransom note. I thought it looked pretty good:

FIX CHARLOTTE OR nEVER SEE PEEBLES AgAIn!

I showed it to Mr. Peebles. He stared at it for a moment, then swiped his paw across the screen, trying to turn the page.

"Wait here," I said. "I'll get you a book."

I ran downstairs to my dad's study and looked over his bookshelf. What would Mr. Peebles like? Something with pictures, maybe. I found one of my old picture books on the bottom shelf. *The Cat in the Hat*. Perfect!

Back in my room, I propped the book on my pillow and set Mr. Peebles in front of it. He sniffed the edges of the book, then rubbed the spine with his chin and licked it.

"You're supposed to read it, not eat it," I said. I opened the book to the middle. Mr. Peebles plopped down on top of the book and began to purr.

"I can see you're a real book lover," I said.

I went back to the ransom note. On second reading, it didn't seem like such a good idea. They would probably guess who sent it, and there was probably some sort of law against catnapping and ransom demands, even if it was for a good cause. Even if the cat was not in fact *napped*, but had defected of his own free will. It wasn't fair.

I could almost hear Mom. *Fair? Life is not fair!* She said that often about things I considered unfair. My mother could be quite unreasonable at times.

My thoughts were interrupted by someone repeatedly pressing our doorbell. I peeked out my window and saw Mrs. Tisk standing on the front steps. My mother answered the door. Words were Spoken, most of them by Mrs. Tisk. Then my mom spoke some Words that made Mrs. Tisk's pasty face turn red, and moments later she turned and walked off all stiff-legged and indignant.

I threw Mr. Peebles in my closet, jumped back in bed, and pretended to be reading something on my tab. A minute later I heard my mother's distinctive, sharp-knuckled rap on my door.

"Yes? Who is it?"

"Ginger, open the door."

I opened the door. My mother's laser-beam eyes instantly zeroed in on the bowl on the floor next to my bed.

"Ginger, why does your room smell like tuna fish?"

"Um . . . I got hungry?"

Her eyes narrowed. "Ginger, did you steal the Tisks' cat?"

"No," I said. It wasn't a lie. Not exactly.

"Do you know where the Tisks' cat is?"

She had me boxed in with that question. I was trying to think what to say when Mr. Peebles started scratching at the closet door.

"It's possible that some strange cat followed me home," I said.

She crossed the room and opened the closet. Mr. Peebles strolled out, hopped onto my bed, and curled up on my pillow.

"Ginger . . . "

"You should ask the Tisks why they messed up my copy of *Charlotte's Web*."

"So that's what this is about. I suppose you think kidnapping is the proper response to a minor computer problem."

"It's not a *minor* problem; it's a *major* one. I mean, how would you like it if somebody changed all the words in one of your books? And it's not *kid*napping, it's *cat*napping, and anyway, I didn't do anything except give Mr. Peebles some tuna."

My mother crossed her arms. "Ginger . . . "

"Nothing can be proved," I said.

"This is not a court of law. I don't need proof to know when my daughter is guilty. I want you to return that cat to the Tisks immediately, if not sooner."

"But what about *Charlotte's Web*?"

"That is a separate issue. Your father said he will deal with it on Monday, and so he will. Now *take that cat back*! And while you're at it, apologize to them."

"But—"

"Now!"

• • •

Mr. Peebles did not care for the cat crate, but I bribed him with some of Barney's cat treats and soon was on my way to the Tisks. Mr. Peebles complained every step of the way.

"Shut up," I told him. "At least you don't have to apologize to that book-wrecking old bag."

"Mroooow!"

"Whatever." I was in no mood to argue. I didn't mind giving the cat back, but I *hated* apologizing to *anybody*—even if I happened to be in the wrong.

Mrs. Tisk opened the door about two seconds after I rang the bell. I saw Dottie standing behind her.

"I found your cat," I said.

"Tsk," she replied.

I opened the crate. Mr. Peebles ran between her legs, into the house, and hopped into Dottie's arms.

"I'm sorry," I said, my jaw almost breaking from the effort of squeezing out those words. "He followed me home."

"Tsk," said Mrs. Tisk.

Mr. Tisk came up behind her. "What is going on here?"

"This is the girl who stole Dottie's cat," said Mrs. Tisk.

Mr. Tisk peered out at me. The two of them filled the doorway. "Oh," he said. "*You.*"

"Yes. Me," I replied. "And I didn't steal him. He followed me home, maybe because he doesn't like living with people who hate books." I probably shouldn't have said that last part, but he was making me mad.

"You are a very rude young lady," said Mrs. Tisk.

"I know you hacked *Charlotte's Web*," I said, getting madder. "And I'm going to prove it!"

She slammed the door in my face—again.

11

The Forgetful Fiancé

The next morning Mom pulled out all the stops for Sunday breakfast: toaster waffles *and* microwaved bacon. Mom and Dad had already finished eating when I got up, but they were still sitting at the table.

"How did it go with the Tisks last night?" Mom asked.

"I gave them their cat back and said I was sorry."

"Good."

"Even though I wasn't, really. After what they did to Charlotte."

"We'll get your book problem straightened out tomorrow," Dad said.

"I'm sure the Tisks did it," I said. "I mean, he *said* he was going to burn every last copy."

"You may be right," Dad said. "But there are

many other possibilities. As I told you before, we'll
get it all straightened out on Monday. You'll just
have to wait."

I am not good at waiting.

I can be a little obsessive sometimes, which is to
say most of the time. There were many things I
could have been doing that day, but the only thing I
wanted was to find out what happens to Charlotte
and Wilbur. If anybody other than my dad could
undo the damage to *Charlotte's Web*, it would
be Billy Bates. Maybe he could help me with the
Flinkwater thing too, if we weren't rudely interrupted again by his tutor.

Given the violently insecticidal tendencies of
his robot butler Alfred, I was relieved when Billy
answered the door himself.

I saw why at once. Alfred was on the floor,
decapitated. Billy was holding his head—or rather,
his sensor array—under his arm.

"You tore Alfred's head off?" I said.

"Just a tune-up," Billy said. He tipped his own
head to the side to look at me from a slightly different angle, as if he was trying to figure out who I
was. "Can I help you?"

That was a weird thing to say. How did he
know I needed help?

"As a matter of fact, yes," I said. "I have a mystery that needs solving. Two mysteries, actually."

"Um . . . okay?" He was still giving me that odd look.

I launched into the whole *Charlotte's Web* thing, and told him about what had happened with the Tisks, and how I'd sort of kidnapped their cat, and how it had all started because I had to write this paper for school, and . . . well, when I get talking, sometimes I talk a lot. I finally ran out of things to say and awaited his hopefully helpful response.

He said, "Okay, but . . . you are . . . who again?"

"I'm still who I've always been," I said. "Are you okay?"

"I'm Billy," he said, not at all helpfully.

"Well I'm Eleanor Roosevelt."

Billy blinked, then said, "Wife of Franklin D. Roosevelt. Longest serving first lady of the United States, March 1933 to April 1945. United States delegate to the United Nations, 1946 through 1952."

I said, "Huh?"

"You seem too young to be *that* Eleanor Roosevelt, whose first name was actually Anna, and who died on November 7, 1962, at age seventy-eight. Were you named after her?"

"No! Billy, cut it out! I was kidding!"

"Your name isn't Eleanor Roosevelt?"

"No!"

"Then what is it?"

I gaped at him uncomprehendingly.

"Seriously," he said. "Have we met?"

I punched him in the stomach.

12

Sherlock

I *know* not to hit people. It's barbaric, rude, dangerous, and unseemly. But then so is pretending not to recognize one's Longtime Acquaintance and Beloved Fiancée and Soul Mate and True Love. Billy was just asking to be punched.

Billy said, "Oof!" and staggered back. "What was that for?"

"For pretending not to recognize me," I said. I felt bad about it right away, even though I didn't hit him that hard. "Are you going to help me or not?"

"Yes! Okay! Just don't do that again."

I unclenched my fist. "It was a one-time thing," I said.

"It *hurt*!"

"I'm sorry."

"You can't just walk into somebody's house

and hit them. And besides, how am I supposed to recognize you? I don't *know* you!"

For the first time, it occurred to me that maybe he wasn't pretending. And that scared me worse than anything.

"I'm *Ginger*!" I said.

"Then why did you tell me your name was Eleanor?"

"I was being sarcastic," I said. "How come you know so much stuff about Eleanor Roosevelt, anyway?"

He shrugged. "I know lots of stuff, especially American history. I have a really good tutor."

Oh-ho, I thought. "You really don't recognize me?"

He shook his head.

"Do you know when Eleanor Roosevelt was born?"

"October 11, 1884. Why?"

Ah-ha, thought I.

"Billy, have you had trouble remembering anything else today?"

"Um . . . not that I know of. Of course, if I can't remember something, then how would I know I don't remember it?"

"Good point. But it's kind of a big deal when you can't remember your girlfriend!"

"I have a girlfriend?"

• • •

It took some convincing. I showed him some of the
selfies we had taken, then we went downstairs to his
subbasement lair and looked up the article about
us in the *Flinkwater Times* from when we saved the
town from the SCIC plague.[6]

"Wow," he said. "I don't remember any of that!
What happened to me?"

"I think you got unREMEMBERed," I said.

Billy thought for a moment, then said, "Oh. It's
like in *A Study in Scarlet*."

"Exactly."

Sherlock Holmes was one of Billy's heroes, along
with Albert Einstein, Alan Turing, and Doctor Who.
I liked Sherlock Holmes too. I had recently read
A Study in Scarlet, in which Dr. Watson discovers
that his friend Holmes doesn't know that the earth
revolves around the sun. Holmes, amused by Watson's
stunned reaction, says, "Now that I do know it I shall
do my best to forget it." Holmes goes on to explain:

I consider that a man's brain originally is like a little empty

attic, and you have to stock it with such furniture as you

choose. . . . There comes a time when for every addition of

knowledge you forget something that you knew before. It is

of the highest importance, therefore, not to have useless facts

elbowing out the useful ones.

---

6 Uh-huh.

Billy said, "My memories of you must've got shoved out of my head when Mr. Rausch downloaded *A Comprehensive History of the United States* into my brain."

"The whole book? How did he do that?"

"I'm not sure," Billy said. "It's all kind of a blur."

"We have to get him to reverse it! Tell him he has to take some of that history out of your head and put me back in."

"But what if my memories are just . . . gone? It's not like you can store memories on a flash drive."

"Isn't that what flash drives *do*?"

"I don't think it's the same. I mean, I don't think you can store feelings and stuff on a chip. Like, I might remember stuff about you, but not why I liked you."

He had a point. If he suddenly remembered everything about me, he might decide he didn't like me after all. But there was lots of good stuff I didn't want him to forget, like our first kiss.

"I bet it's all still in there," I said. "Like the memories got compressed and stuck in some corner of your brain to make room for all that history. We just have to figure out how to unlock the files. We have to call Mr. Rausch."

"Okay . . . but what if to fit you back into my head he has to take out something really important?"

I almost punched him again. But I didn't.

13

Gilly

Reaching Mr. Rausch turned out to be impossible. The only contact info Billy had for him was an old-fashioned e-mail address. I mean, who checks their e-mail?

Billy typed an urgent-sounding note and hit send. While we were waiting for a reply, I took the opportunity to tell him as many good things about myself as I could remember.

"For one thing, I introduced you to your dad," I said. "Do you remember meeting Gilly?" Gilly, aka Billy's dad, had mysteriously disappeared when Billy was a toddler, and just turned up a few months ago to reclaim his position.

"Yes!" he said. "It was at the Crump's house. Gilly was friends with Mr. and Mrs. Crump, and he looked like a Sasquatch!"

"Yeah, he'd been living in the woods for ten

years. Do you remember me being there?"

Billy knit his brow and thought. "I think there was a girl. . . . "

"Yes! Me!"

"It's kind of fuzzy."

I hoped he wasn't talking about my hair.

"Do you remember when we escaped from jail?" I asked.

He scrunched his brow. "You were there?"

I wanted to scream, but I held it in.

"I'm sorry," he said. "It's all a blank."

"What did that tutor *do* to you?"

"I don't exactly remember that, either. We were talking about the history book, and there were wires involved, and some sort of machine. The next thing I knew, my head was full of history and I never even had to read anything."

"I don't see how that's possible," I said.

"Well, this *is* Flinkwater."

"True. Flinkwater should be named Strangetown, or maybe Weirdville. It would make my assignment easier, that's for sure."

"Assignment?"

"I'm supposed to write about why Flinkwater is called Flinkwater. I told you all about that yesterday."

"Sorry. Don't remember."

"You know what really bugs me? How come you forgot *me*? Why not just forget your last few games of Interzone Apocalypse?"

"No! I've got over twelve trillion Interzone Crowns, and I'm a Third-Degree Zone Mage!"

"You're a third-degree idiot," I said, more than a little miffed that his IA score seemed to mean more to him than our Eternal Love.

"Tell me again how come I like you?" he said. I must have been clenching my fists again, because he quickly added, "Kidding! Just kidding!"

"It's okay," I said, forcing myself to relax. "I just don't like to think of myself as forgettable."

We were interrupted by a metallic clatter and a startled exclamation from upstairs.

"That sounds like Gilly," Billy said.

"We'd better tell him what's happened."

We ran up the stairs and found Gilly sitting on the floor in the front hall reattaching Alfred's head to his torso.

"Don't you know you're not supposed to leave disassembled robots lying where someone could trip over them?" he said.

"Sorry. I was reprogramming him when I got interrupted," Billy said.

"Why were you reprogramming Alfred?"

"He's got this little glitch." Billy pointed at

the damaged wall. "He punches holes in things."

"Oh. Yes. That." Gilly stood and lifted Alfred back onto his motilators.

Alfred and Gilly made an odd-looking couple. Gilly was tall and gangly with big features—like a beardless Abraham Lincoln, if you can imagine Lincoln in baggy shorts, flip-flops, and a Hawaiian shirt. Being the founder and chief executive officer of an international high-tech company such as ACPOD comes with certain benefits like a private jet and oodles of money. But to Gilbert Bates, the most important benefit was that he could wear shorts and flip-flops to work.

Alfred, of course, was a robot.

"Are you online, Alfred?" Gilly asked.

Alfred rotated his sensor array 360 degrees. I took a step back, just in case.

"Thank you, sir. I am fully functional."

"Excellent. Tea. Earl Grey. Hot."

"Very good, sir." Alfred motilated off toward the kitchen to make tea.

"Dad, we have a problem," Billy said.

"I'm sure Alfred will be fine," Gilly said.

"Alfred's not the problem. It's that tutor you hired for me."

"You mean Ernie Rausch?"

"Yeah," I jumped in. "He filled up Billy's head

with history, and now Billy doesn't even remember me."

Gilly looked from Billy to me with a puzzled expression. "Billy doesn't remember you?"

"No!"

"Oh . . . umm . . . and who are you exactly?"

That was when things went from irritating and weird to flat-out scary. Because it's bad enough to be forgotten by your boyfriend. Boys, after all, are notorious for that sort of thing. But to be forgotten by *everybody* . . . TOTALLY UNACCEPTABLE!

And, frankly, terrifying.

"I'm *GINGER!*" I shrieked.

Seriously, it was a *shriek*. Both Gilly and Billy jumped back in alarm.

"Of course you are," said Gilly in the sort of voice you might use to calm a suicide bomber.

"I'm *Ginger Crump*," I said in a slightly more reasonable tone, "and you've known me for months."

"Crump," Gilly said. "Do you belong to Royce and Amanda Crump?"

"I don't *belong* to anyone. They're my parents."

"It's true," Billy said. "She showed me selfies of us and everything, but my memory of her is gone, same as yours."

Alfred rolled up, carrying a tray with a

porcelain cup balanced upon it. "Your tea, sir."

Gilly took the cup. I noticed his hand was shaking.

Alfred pointed his sensor array at me. "Ms. Crump, would you care for a beverage?"

At least the robot hadn't forgotten me.

"No thank you, Alfred."

Gilly said, "Alfred, has Ms. Crump visited us before?"

"On eight occasions since I came online, sir."

"Was I present?"

"Yes, sir, on three of those occasions."

"So it's true," Gilly touched the side of his chin with a long forefinger. "I am experiencing some form of selective amnesia. I wonder what else is missing."

"Do you remember when you were the Sasquatch of Flinkwater Park?"

"Certainly . . . although I wasn't a *real* Sasquatch."

"Did Mr. Rausch do some sort of memory thing to you?" I asked.

"He helped me remember the entire code sequence on the antigravity dro—" Gilly stopped talking abruptly and shot me a look.

"It's okay," I said. "I know all about the secret antigravity drone you're working on."

"You do?" he said.

"Billy told me."

"I did?" Billy said.

"Don't worry, you can trust me. I've known you since you were a Sasquatch."

Gilly nodded thoughtfully. "Alfred!" he said.

"Sir?"

"Get Ernest Rausch on the phone, please."

Alfred buzzed and blinked. A few seconds later, Mr. Rausch's voice issued from Alfred's speaker.

"Hello?"

"Rausch, this is Gilbert Bates."

"Oh! Hello, Mr. Bates," said Mr. Rausch.

"I'm having a little problem. I seem to have forgotten something."

"I can help! What is it you want to remember?"

"If I could remember what I don't remember, I wouldn't have a problem now, would I?"

"Of course! I'm sure it's a minor adjustment to your dynamic engram interface. Can you meet me at the neuroprosthetics lab? I can be there in half an hour."

"The sooner the better," Gilly said. "I'm on my way."

14

Webhound

Billy wanted to go, but Gilly told him to stay home.

"Let me find out exactly what happened. If Rausch can restore my memories successfully, then we'll see what he can do for you. In any case, just to be safe, I'm shutting down the REMEMBER program. We can't have people losing memories willy-nilly. If I've forgotten Jennifer here—"

"Ginger!" I said.

"Yes, Ginger. Sorry. If I've forgotten you, then who knows what else I've forgotten?"

"My dad forgot we have a cat," I said.

"And your father is . . . ?"

"Royce Crump!"

"Oh, that's right."

"I think you should go see Mr. Rausch," I said.

• • •

After Gilly left, I asked Billy to help me with *Charlotte's Web*. He might not remember that he was in love with me, but he was still a boy genius. I explained what had happened, and how I suspected the Tisks were behind it.

It took him only a few minutes to find the problem. Sort of.

"All the digital files have been corrupted," he reported.

"Way to go, Sherlock," I said sarcastically. "Like I didn't figure that out on my own!"

"No," he said. "I mean, *all* the files. Not just your tablet, and not just the Flinkwater County Library system. Every library in the country got hit. Even the source files at the publisher have been replaced with this edited version. In other words, the original *Charlotte's Web* no longer exists. Somebody wrote a really nasty little worm, like a computer version of the Ebola virus, only worse. The Net is saturated with it. Anybody who has an unaltered copy of *Charlotte's Web* on their device loses it the instant they access the Net. It's quite brilliant, actually. You say Mr. Tisk is behind it? I thought he was a preacher."

"He threatened to get rid of every last copy of *Charlotte's Web*, so yeah, I'd say he's our number one suspect."

"I don't see an IP address at his house . . . or at his church, either. I don't see how he could create a virus like this without being plugged into the Web."

"Maybe he hired some hacker to do it for him."

Billy nodded. "Let me see what I can find."

Watching Billy on his computer was like seeing a movie in fast motion. Screen after screen flickered by; I really couldn't follow what he was doing. After a few minutes he slumped back in his chair.

"I tracked the virus back to an ACPOD server here in Flinkwater, but from there it leads to a cascading series of proxies—basically, just about every IP address within five hundred miles of here, with Flinkwater as the geographical center. Whoever did this is local, and they're good. It's like looking for a needle the size of an eyelash in a haystack the size of Iowa."

"So there's no way to prove who did it?"

"Eventually. I sent a webhound after it."

"Webhound?"

"A tracking program I wrote. But it might take a few hours. Or maybe longer, like a few days, if it has to chew through a lot of firewalls.

"How do we fix *Charlotte's Web* in the meantime?" I asked.

"We can't. It's gone."

"Gone?"

"Gone."

"What about paper books? If we had a paper copy of *Charlotte's Web* we could scan it and create a new digital file, right?"

Billy touched the side of his chin with his forefinger. I loved when he did that, even though I knew he'd stolen the gesture from his dad.

"I suppose we could do a reverse hack. Hack the hacker. But where would we get a paper copy? A museum?"

"Flinkwater Memorial Library," I said.

"Seriously? I thought that got turned into an old-folks home."

"Well, a lot of old folks do hang out there," I said. "But it's closed today, so we can't get in."

Billy grinned. I'd seen that expression before.

Billy used to have a collection of magnetic key cards that gave him access to just about every building in Flinkwater. But back when we got arrested for treason by the Department of Homeland Security, they had confiscated his collection.

"I thought the DHS took your key cards," I said.

"They did, so I made something better. Check it out." He sorted through the junk on his desk and came up with what looked like an old-fashioned oversize wristwatch. "I took the guts out and put in an RFID transmitter, smart-mag technology, and a titanium lock pick. I call it the Open Anything Watch. You ready?"

"I don't know. . . . " I'd been to jail once. I didn't like it.

"You want to read *Charlotte's Web* or not? It's not like we'd be doing anything wrong."

"Breaking and entering? Stealing a book? Ms. Pfleuger will kill us if we get caught."

"We won't break anything, and you'd just be *borrowing* the book. That's what libraries are for, right?"

I thought it over for about three seconds. I really did want to read the rest of *Charlotte's Web*.

15

Breaking and Entering

Billy was disappointed by the lock on the front door of the library.

"It's just a lock," he said.

It was the old-fashioned type that required a metal key. He'd been hoping for something high-tech so he could show off his Open Anything Watch.

"Does this mean you have to give your watch a new name?" I asked.

"No, it just means it's going to be harder than I thought." He took off the watch and extracted a long, flexible metal strip from the band. "Lock pick. This might take a few minutes."

On an impulse, I reached past him and twisted the doorknob. The latch clicked and the door swung open. Billy looked at me, astonished.

"How did you do that?"

"Magic."

"Yeah, right."

"Or maybe Ms. Pfleuger forgot to lock it," I said as we slipped through the door into the empty library. The air was dead still; motes of dust hovered nearly motionless in the air, lit up by the sun coming through the windows. Billy looked around at the shelves of books.

"Wow, that's a lot of paper."

"You've never been here before?"

"Not since I was a little kid. Where are the computers? How are we going to find the book you want?"

I pointed out the COMPUTER-FREE ZONE sign on the back wall. "I think the book will be in the children's section." I started toward the corner where they kept the kids' books, but was stopped by the most chilling sound imaginable—that of my name being spoken by a large, largely insane librarian.

"Ginger Crump!"

I froze. Ms. Pfleuger, wearing a dark green muumuu decorated with red and gold snakes, rose up from behind her desk like Godzilla rising from the ocean.

"The library is closed," she said, coming toward us. As she got closer, I could see that what I'd thought were red and gold snakes were actually strings of flowers printed on her dress. Which did not make her any less scary—snakes, flowers . . . she still looked like Godzilla.

"The door was open!" I squeaked. At least it sounded squeaky to me.

"We didn't do anything!" Billy was sounding a little squeaky too.

The Pformidable Pfleuger fixed her flame-thrower eyes on us.

"Why. Are. You. Here?" she inquired terrifyingly.

"I want to check out a book!" I shrieked. Okay, it wasn't really a shriek, but it was close.

Ms. Pfleuger halted her advance. The fire in her eyes abated.

"I thought you didn't like books," she said.

"I do! I do like books! I *love* books!"

Ms. Pfleuger crossed her arms and regarded us suspiciously.

"Seriously," I said. "I was hoping I could check out *Charlotte's Web*."

"I thought you intended to read that . . . *electronically*." She practically spat out that last word.

"I was, but there's sort of a problem."

"Oh?" She cocked her head and waited for more.

"The e-book got hacked." I showed her some of the altered text on my tab. "It's not just my tab; it's everywhere." As Ms. Pfleuger listened, I saw a grim smile spread slowly across her face. She *liked* that the e-books had been corrupted.

"We think the Tisks did it," I said.

"The Tisks?" That seemed to make her even happier.

"We haven't *proved* it was the Tisks," Billy said. "But we're pretty sure it was somebody in Flinkwater."

"But we can fix it," I said. "We just need a hard copy of Charlotte so we can scan it and unhack the hack."

"I see. So it seems *real* books are important after all?" She loomed over us triumphantly.

"Yes! I was wrong!"

"Important enough for you to break into my library? We're closed on Sunday, you know."

"We didn't actually break anything," I said. "The door was open. Er . . . how come you're here, anyway?"

"That is not your concern. In any case, your felonious efforts have gone for naught. Our only copy of *Charlotte's Web* is checked out."

"No!" I couldn't believe it. "By who?"

"*Whom,*" said Ms. Pfleuger.

"*Whom* checked it out?"

"*Who,*" said Ms. Pfleuger.

I will *never* understand that who/whom business!

Ms. Pfleuger said, "I'm afraid I can't share information about our patrons' library records."

"But what about all those kids all across the country who are right this minute reading *Charlotte's Web* on their tabs, and instead of a spider and a pig talking, it's a couple of humans? We need to fix this!"

That made an impression. Ms. Pfleuger thought for a moment, then said, "Mycroft Duchakis was here yesterday afternoon."

"Myke? Myke has Charlotte?"

"I really can't say," she said, looking away.

I turned to Billy, but he had wandered off and was standing over by Ms. Pfleuger's desk.

"I thought this was supposed to be a computer-free zone," he said.

"Get away from there!" Ms. Pfleuger snapped.

Billy backed away from her desk.

"I think it's time for you two to leave," Ms. Pfleuger said in a firm voice.

That sounded like a good idea to me. I grabbed Billy and pulled him toward the exit, but not before I got a glimpse of the D-Monix 15395 computer on Ms. Pfleuger's desk.

"Out!" she commanded, thrusting a forefinger at the door.

We got out.

"Now what?" Billy asked.

"Myke Duchakis has Charlotte! At least I think that's what she was telling us. I'm going over there."

"I should probably check on my webhound program and see if it's chewed through all those proxies yet."

"Okay, you do that, and I'll go get the book from Myke."

We took off in opposite directions.

16

Myke Duchakis

Dark-skinned, rotund Myke Duchakis came from his room, bearing a basket of sleeping multicolored kittens.

"Oh," he said, "I thought you were Mrs. Gumm."

"Do I *look* like Mrs. Gumm?" Addy Gumm was the town's cat lady, and she was a thousand years old at least.

"Not really," Myke said. "Umm . . . do you want a kitten?"

"No thanks. How many do you have there?"

"I'm not actually sure. At least six. Possibly eight. They're exhausted from terrorizing my chinchilla. He's in his exercise ball, quivering with fear."

One of the kittens—a black one—raised its head and said "Eep?"

"Are you sure you don't want one?"

"Pretty sure," I said. They *were* awfully cute.

"Did you know that cats were considered sacred by the ancient Egyptians?"

"I did not know that," I said.

Myke is crazy for all kinds of animals. He is the founder and president of AAPT, which stands for Animals Are People Too. He volunteers at Clawz-n-Pawz, our local animal adoption agency.

Myke's adoptive parents have lived in Flinkwater forever—his dad used to play for the Flinkwater Brazen Bulls, our high school football team, and he now coaches them. Myke's mom grew up on a farm near Halibut, but Myke's biological parents were from northern Africa. He likes to think of himself as a royal descendent of the Egyptian pharaohs. Whatever you do, don't get him started on the Sphinx—he'll talk your ears off.

"They used to mummify the pharaoh's pet cats," he said. "That way when the pharaoh died, he would have a friend waiting for him in the afterlife." One of the kittens had crawled out of the basket and was climbing up Myke's shirt. "Mrs. Gumm promised to take one of the kittens. And Ernie Rausch might take one, but I still need homes for the rest of them."

"Ernie Rausch? Are you talking about *Ernest* Rausch, the memory expert?"

"Yeah, Ernie's a member of AAPT. He used to

work in Area 51—you know, that horrible animal-experimentation program ACPOD shut down a couple months ago? Anyway, he says he misses the animals, so he's taking a lot of them and keeping them at his farm—animals nobody else will adopt. You know that place just north of town? Happy Smile?

"I've seen the sign." It was hard to miss: a giant, white-toothed, pink-lipped, disembodied grin with HAPPY SMILE ACRES arched across the top.

"Ernie's dad was a dentist, but he's gone now, so it's just Ernie and a bunch of animals. Only he swears he doesn't experiment on them. He just keeps them because he likes them. He says they make him more creative." Myke looked at the pile of kittens in his arms. "I'm hoping he'll take two. I'd keep them myself but my mom, she thinks it's getting kind of crowded here."

I couldn't blame her. Last time I visited Myke he had a chinchilla, a monkey, three mice, a pigeon, a gecko, and a three-legged squirrel in his bedroom.

"I met Mr. Rausch's dog yesterday," I said.

"Which one?"

"A bulldog named Gertrude."

"Oh yeah. She was a rescue. Nice dog."

"Speaking of animals, I heard you checked out *Charlotte's Web* from the library. I was wondering if I could borrow it."

"You want to borrow my borrowed book?" He gently detached the kitten from his shirt and put it back in the basket. "How come all of a sudden everybody wants to read *Charlotte's Web*?"

"What do you mean 'everybody'?"

"Well, you and Dottie."

"Dottie? Dottie *Tisk*?"

"Yeah, she volunteers at Clawz-n-Pawz too. She asked me to check it out for her."

That made sense. If Mr. Tisk had taken the book from her before she finished reading it, Dottie might want it back.

"Dottie will have to wait," I said. "I need it right now. It's an emergency."

"Too late. I already gave it to her."

17

Dottie Tisk

Dottie Tisk had the library's only copy of *Charlotte's Web*. That was the worst possible situation. If her parents found it, they'd destroy it. If I went to their house and asked Dottie if I could borrow it, she might deny she had it. But I had to try. The Tisks lived just a few houses away, so I headed over there.

The Jesus statue was standing guard, of course. I avoided his eyes, but as I passed, I said, "Don't worry, I'm not going to do anything bad."

No one answered the door. I should've known—they were probably at Glorious Heart, Mr. Tisk's church, being it was Sunday and all. I peeked in through the front window. An ordinary living room—no *Charlotte's Web* in sight. I looked back at the statue. It hadn't turned its head or anything spooky, so I walked around the house and checked out some of the other windows.

Dottie's bedroom was at the back of the house. Her window was behind some rosebushes. I eased between the thorny bushes and the house. Her window was open a crack. I pushed the window up far enough to poke my head through and looked around. The room was incredibly neat and boring — nothing hanging on the walls, no clothes strewn on the floor, no *Charlotte's Web* or any other books. I hiked the front half of my body onto the sill and took a closer look. She had probably hidden the book from her parents. I inched farther in so just my legs were sticking out of the window.

Something furry and gray exploded from the floor and flew past me through the open window. I was so startled I fell into the room.

"Come back here!" I yelled.

Mr. Peebles was about to do no such thing. He was over the fence and gone in an instant.

"Not my fault," I muttered. Even though it clearly *was* my fault, saying it wasn't made me feel better. As long as I was in Dottie's room — also not my fault — I decided to take a look around.

From what I could see, Dottie was the neatest, most boring fourteen-year-old girl on the planet. Her bed was so perfectly made it looked like something out of a virtual-reality set.

Where would a neat freak hide a book? I looked

through all the drawers. I checked her closet with its precisely hung row of stodgy dresses. I looked under her bed. Not so much as a single dust bunny.

I heard voices, then the sound of the bedroom door opening. I scooted under the bed. I could see Dottie's feet.

"Mom!" she shouted. A moment later I saw Mrs. Tisk's white shoes enter the room.

"Mr. Peebles is gone!" Dottie said.

"Tsk—you left your window open," Mrs. Tisk said.

"I did not! It was only open a crack when I left."

Mrs. Tisk crossed over to the window and closed it.

"Mr. Peebles must have got it open," Dottie said.

"That cat is freakishly smart," Mrs. Tisk said. "He's more trouble than he's worth. If he returns, we're giving him back to your uncle."

"Nooo!" Dottie wailed.

I heard a *thwack* and a gasp. I was pretty sure Dottie had just gotten slapped.

"Control yourself!" Mrs. Tisk snapped. "Do not contradict your elders. You will stay in this room until I decide it's time for you to come out!" She marched out of the room and slammed the door.

Dottie let out a tiny sob and sat down on her bed. After a few more sobs she knelt down next to the bed. Her knees were inches from my face. Was she praying? No, she was pulling something out from between the mattress and the box spring. She stood up and plopped onto the bed. A moment later I heard the dry, slithery sound of paper pages being turned.

Charlotte! I was sure of it. She was reading *Charlotte's Web*!

I would have to wait for Dottie to leave, then grab the book and escape through the window—but judging by the tone her mother had taken, that could be hours. I eased my cell out of my pocket and texted Billy.

> Help! Stuck under Dottie's bed and she is sitting on it.
> Need distraction.

I hit send. My phone made a whoosh sound—I'd forgotten to mute it. Had Dottie heard? I held my breath. Dottie was moving around. I watched for her feet to hit the floor, but instead it was her hair that landed on the carpet, framing her upside-down face like a curtain. Her colorless eyes regarded me with the cold, unblinking detachment of a boa constrictor.

"Hey," I said friendlily.

"You are under my bed," she said unfriendlily.

"True." There was no point in denying it.

"You left my window open," she said.

"It was already a little bit open," I said. "I just opened it a little more."

"Why do you keep stealing Mr. Peebles?" Her face was turning red. I thought for a second it was because she was mad, but then I decided it was because she was hanging upside down.

"Mr. Peebles has a mind of his own."

"Why are you here?"

"Because of *Charlotte's Web*," I said.

She stared at me without replying.

"Your parents wrecked my e-book. They made a computer virus that messed up every digital copy of *Charlotte's Web* on the planet. I need to borrow the book so I can fix it."

Dottie's head retracted. I wriggled out from under the bed. She was sitting against the headboard hugging the copy of Charlotte to her chest.

"You can't have it. I'm not done."

"You're not even supposed to be reading it," I said.

"And you're not supposed to be breaking into people's houses stealing their cats."

"That was an accident! Anyway, if you call your parents, I'll tell them you're reading Charlotte."

I had her there—I could tell by the way she scowled.

"My parents don't even have a computer," Dottie said. "They couldn't do what you said even if they wanted to."

"Maybe they got somebody else to do it for them."

Dottie's dead eyes flickered at that. She knew something she wasn't telling me.

"We're going to track down whoever did it," I said. "Billy Bates has a webhound on the digital trail, and I bet it leads right here."

Dottie laughed. It sounded like rusty bedsprings. I guessed she hadn't had much practice.

"You won't be laughing when I have your parents arrested." I said that mostly because I was mad, not because I thought I could actually do it.

Dottie's face turned red. "You better not. You think losing your stupid e-book is bad, what if . . . whoever did it . . . what if . . . oh never mind." She looked away. "It's just one stupid book. What if you forgot everything you ever read? How would you like that?"

I said, "Huh?"

My cell chirped. It was Billy.

You still stuck?

I texted back.

No.

Billy replied a second later.

Get over here now.

I hesitated. Did he mean "as soon as is convenient" or "*NOW* now"? I texted back.

Getting book. Be there in a while.

"Who are you talking to?" Dottie asked.

"None of your business. Look, Dottie, I really need that book. I promise I'll return it to you tomorrow."

"No! I want to know what happens."

"You can wait. This is important!"

Dottie shoved the book under her butt and crossed her arms. This was not going well.

I said, in my most reasonable voice, "Dottie, you—"

My cell chirped again. It was Billy.

NOW!!!

"Dottie!" Mrs. Tisk's voice came from outside the room. "Who are you talking to?"

I was out the window in a flash. It was an impressive exit—except for the part where I landed in the rosebushes, then snagged my favorite jeans on the way over the fence and tore a huge hole in the knee. Scratched, irritated, and a bit shredded, I headed for Billy's house.

18

The Drone

Alfred let me in.

"Master Billy is in the backyard," he informed me. I followed him through the house and out a set of French doors to where Billy and Gilly were sitting on the patio watching a black disk hovering three feet above the lawn. Billy was holding a tablet in his lap. He moved his fingers over the surface of the tab, and the disk rose several feet higher.

"Nice drone," I said.

Billy's hand jerked; the disk tipped and did a nosedive into a flower bed.

"Sorry," Billy said to his father.

"Don't worry," Gilly said. "The AG-3601 is quite durable, but the control interface is touchy." He took the tab from Billy. The drone rose from the flower bed, swooped toward us, and settled on the patio.

Billy said, "Pretty cool, huh?"

"It looks like a flying manhole cover," I said. "Is *that* what you texted me about?" I was a bit irritated. Not that the antigravity drone wasn't cool, but I was focused on Charlotte, and I didn't like having my mission interrupted. "Did you find the source of the book hacking, or have you been playing dronemaster?"

"Never mind the book," Billy said. "We've got bigger problems." He looked intently at his father. "Dad, do you remember Ginger?"

"Certainly," Gilly said. "Hello, Ginger." He looked at my torn jeans. "Is that the new fashion these days?"

"It's what everybody's wearing," I said. "I'm glad you got your memory back."

"There's nothing wrong with my memory." He looked at Billy. "I really don't know why you keep going on about it."

Billy said, "Do you remember when Ginger was here this morning, and you didn't remember her at all?"

"Do you mean do I remember not remembering Ginger? How could I not remember Ginger?" He smiled at me. "Ginger is very memorable."

"Tell us what you were doing this afternoon."

"Why, I was at the office."

"And why did you go to work on a Sunday afternoon?"

Gilly shrugged. "I can't say I recall."

"And what did you do while you were there?"

"Several things, I'm sure."

"Did you see Mr. Rausch?"

"Possibly. Who is he again?"

Billy looked at me. I looked at Billy. We both looked at Gilly, who seemed blissfully unconcerned.

"I can be a bit absentminded when I'm working on a project," he admitted. "Did I miss a dental appointment or something?"

"This is serious," Billy said. "Rausch did something to Gilly's brain."

"He did something to your brain too, don't forget." We were in Billy's room. Gilly was still on the patio working on the AG-3601 interface.

"At least I haven't forgotten that I don't remember you," he said.

"That makes me feel so much better."

Billy said, "It's not all bad news. We know the process is reversible, because this morning Gilly didn't remember you at all, and now he does—but he's forgotten who Mr. Rausch is."

"Why would Rausch wipe himself out of your dad's memory?"

"Gilly said he wanted to shut down the REMEMBER program, remember? I bet Rausch made him forget that to save his job. It looks like he's deliberately stealing people's memories."

"But why? Why would he bother to steal *your* memories of *me*? It doesn't make sense."

"I suppose we could ask him."

"We have to ask him sneakily," I said. "Myke told me Rausch has a farm north of town. Happy Smile Acres. Maybe we should pay him a visit."

"A sneaky visit?"

"Very sneaky."

19

WheelBots

Going on a secret reconnaissance mission required a new look, especially since my jeans were shredded, so I went home for a quick change.

Mom was gone. Dad was in his reading chair with Dr. Moreau and, to my utter astonishment, Mr. Peebles.

This was remarkable not because Mr. Peebles had found his way to our house—after all, he knew he could get tuna fish—but because my father did not like cats. He and Barney barely tolerated each other, and here he was with Mr. Peebles nestled in his arms, the two of them happily reading a book.

Then things got even weirder.

"I didn't know Barney liked to read," he said.

I took a moment to blink and let my mouth fall open.

"Dad . . . that's not Barney."

He looked at the cat. "Are you sure?"

"Of course I'm sure! Barney is a Siamese! That's Mr. Peebles!"

"We have two cats?"

"Dad!"

"Ginger, you can't expect me to keep track of every stray animal that walks through the house."

"Dad, this is serious. I think your memory has been hacked."

"Hacked?"

"Hacked right out of your head! By the memory guy, Mr. Rausch. You're not the only one forgetting things. Billy and Gilly both completely forgot who I am."

"Ginger, that's ridiculous." He set his book aside. Mr. Peebles jumped down and trotted off. "Why would Mr. Rausch want anyone to forget you?"

"I don't know! Why would he want to steal your memory of *Barney*? I mean, who knows what else you guys have forgotten? And you said a lot of the engineers at ACPOD are forgetting things too!"

"That is true." He frowned. "I wonder if it could be an unintended side effect of Rausch's REMEMBER technique."

"What is his technique? I mean, what exactly does he *do*?"

My father scrunched his brow and slowly shook his head.

"I can't seem to remember," he said. "What happened to your jeans?"

"I don't remember," I said. "Can I borrow your WheelBot?"

I changed into black leggings, a matching T-shirt, and a pair of black sneakers. It made me feel very mysterious and ninja, perfect for a super-sneaky recon mission, even if it was the middle of the day. I rolled Dad's self-propelled, gyroscopically-controlled unicycle out of the garage and sped down the street at top speed—about the same as an easy jog, but far less tiring. ACPOD has been making WheelBots for years, but they haven't caught on. Probably because they make you look ridiculous— like you're balancing yourself on a beach ball. I don't use Dad's WheelBot very often, but Happy Smile Acres was five miles away. Besides, I looked like a ninja, and a ninja would look cool even riding on a donkey. I did wish Dad's WheelBot wasn't painted pink and green, but what can you do?

Billy was waiting for me outside his house on his own WheelBot. He was wearing orange shorts and a yellow shirt—not exactly inconspicuous. But his WheelBot was ninja black.

"You want to trade?" I asked. "For fashion consistency?"

"Better not. My bot's kind of touchy. I made some modifications."

I didn't argue. When Billy says he "made some modifications," it could mean anything from "laser-cannon headlamps" to "ejection seat."

The police get touchy about unicycles on the highway, so we took the county road out of town. After half a mile we turned up a dirt road. Fields of twelve-foot-tall drying cornstalks formed golden walls on either side of us.

Billy said, "Watch this."

He leaned forward and twisted his handgrip. His WheelBot produced a high-pitched whine and took off, leaving me coughing and spitting in a cloud of dust. Seconds later, when the dust had cleared, I saw Billy a quarter mile ahead of me, looking back and waving.

"Show off," I muttered grittily. I accelerated to my maximum speed of twelve miles per hour.

"It'll do forty miles per hour," he said when I caught up with him.

"Good for you," I said, both irritated and impressed. Billy had never met a machine he couldn't make faster, smarter, or more dangerous.

"Sorry about the dust."

"Just don't do it again." We continued up the road at a more reasonable pace, riding side by side.

"By the way, since you haven't bothered to ask, Dottie has the book."

"Oh! Did you get it?"

"No. But I'm pretty sure she knows who hacked the e-book."

"She told you that?"

"Not exactly, but she knows something. I think her father hired somebody to do the hacking. I was about to get it out of her when you texted."

"Sorry. I was kind of freaked out when Gilly got home. He was acting so weird. He had the AG-3601 with him, and when I asked him why he'd brought it home, he said he couldn't remember. And then that whole thing about not remembering Mr. Rausch . . . it was scary."

"It's *still* scary."

We made two more turns. The farm roads around Flinkwater are like a gigantic corn maze; tourists have been known to get lost in them for hours.

"What are we going to do once we get there?" Billy asked.

"Scope it out. If he's not home, we'll take a look around, maybe find some clues as to how he does his memory trick."

"And if he *is* home?"

"Then we go to plan B, the frontal approach. I'll talk to him. You can be my backup. I mean, it's not like he's going to take me prisoner. Right?"

20

Happy Smiles

Happy Smile Acres did not look happy, and it did not make me smile. The sign, about half the size of a billboard, desperately needed a fresh coat of paint, as did the farmhouse, the barn, and the out-buildings. The whole place was surrounded by a six-foot chain-link fence. It looked like a prison set in the middle of a cornfield.

Billy and I rolled up the short driveway and peered through the gate.

"I don't see a car or anything," Billy said. "Maybe he's not home."

"All the better for snooping," I said. "We can stash our wheels in the cornfield."

"The gate's locked," he said doubtfully.

"Since when did a lock stop *you*?"

We climbed off our WheelBots and went to examine the large padlock securing the gate. "No problem," he said after a moment. "Except . . . "

I looked where he was pointing.

"Over by the corner of the barn," he said.

I saw it. An exceptionally large, exceptionally black bull was staring at us with a look so baleful and malevolent I could feel it in my intestines.

"Is that . . . ?"

"It sure looks like him," Billy said.

The bull's name was Brazie, and he had once served as the live mascot for the Brazen Bulls, Flinkwater High's pathetic football team.

"I thought he was dead."

"He doesn't *look* dead."

Three years ago, when Brazie was just a calf, he got the job of romping around the football field wearing a blue-and-gold cape at the start of every game. He was a big hit at first. But Brazie got bigger, as bulls do, and sprouted a set of horns, as bulls will. He became less interested in comical romping and more interested in charging and trampling. Brazie's last appearance on the Flinkwater High football field resulted in Coach Duchakis being head-butted into the stands, breaking his collarbone, and suffering a serious puncture wound to his gluteus maximus.

Brazie was fired from his position. We all thought he'd been sent to a slaughterhouse in Des Moines, but here he was, bigger and meaner-looking than ever.

"Myke told me Mr. Rausch adopts a lot of dogs and cats. I guess he adopts bulls, too."

Billy pulled out his cell and started poking at the screen.

"What are you doing?" I asked.

"Plan C," he said. "Watch." He pointed at the horizon in the direction of Flinkwater.

I looked but didn't see anything except a few fluffy clouds and a bright blue sky.

"It should be here in about ninety seconds."

"What is 'it'?"

"Just wait." Ninety seconds later I saw a small dark dot. I thought it was a bird at first, but no bird ever flew that fast. The dot grew rapidly larger, coming straight at us, and a second later I could make out the disklike shape of the AG-3601 prototype. The drone slowed as it approached, then stopped a few yards away from us, hovering belly high off the ground. "Ta-da!" Billy said.

"You called it here on your phone?"

"I downloaded the codes off Gilly's tab and disabled the security protocols. All we have to do is attach a camera, and we've got ourselves a surveillance drone."

"You have a camera?"

"We've got your phone. I figure we can attach it to the bottom, then set up a video call to my phone."

I squatted down so I could see the bottom of

the drone. "I don't see any way to attach it."

Billy opened the small storage compartment on his WheelBot and took out a roll of duct tape. "Never leave home without it. Give me your cell."

I gave him my phone and watched as he got underneath the hovering drone. Before he could apply the tape, the drone wobbled and started moving away from us.

"Uh-oh." Billy quickly made some adjustments on his cell. "Gilly might be trying to take control." He ran his fingers over the display; the drone returned to its original position, but it was still wobbling back and forth like a little kid with a full bladder. "He must be using a signal booster. Can you hold it steady while I tape the phone on?"

Rather nervously I grasped the rim of the drone. It was surprisingly warm and very wiggly.

"Hold it still!" Billy said from beneath the drone.

"I'm trying!"

"Put some weight on it; I think that'll help."

I reached over the top, grabbed the far side of the disk, and put the weight of the top half of my body on it. My toes were barely touching the ground.

"That's better. Hang on."

"I'm hanging!" I really *was* hanging—the drone had elevated itself a few more inches and was supporting my entire weight.

"Okay, I think I got it."

The drone was rising.

"You can get off now," he said.

"Off? Are you kidding?" The drone was still going up. Looking over the edge, I could see Billy's face ten feet below.

"Hang on, I'll bring it back down. Don't fall."

"Hurry!" I did not suffer from acrophobia, or fear of heights, but neither was I stupid or suicidal. I pulled myself forward so I was clamped onto the disk with both my arms and my legs. Below me, Billy was frantically working his cell.

"I got it," he said. "Hang on, let me just—"

The drone shot straight up into the sky, with me, screaming, on top of it.

21

Acrophobia

You know that uncomfortable feeling you get going up in a fast elevator? Multiply that by a thousand. You know that scary floating-stomach feeling you get when the elevator stops? Multiply it by a million.

The drone stopped abruptly, almost throwing me off. I think I screamed again, but I couldn't hear myself over the roar of my pounding pulse.

Remember when I said I wasn't acrophobic? I changed my mind. Looking down at Billy's tiny face eighty feet below me, I was in an utter panic. So I screamed some more.

"Hang on!" Billy shouted. "Don't fall!"

"STOP SAYING THAT!" I yelled. At least the drone wasn't moving.

"That was Gilly trying to regain control of the AG-3601." Billy's voice was coming from the phone he'd taped to the bottom of the drone. "I've got him locked out now. Just don't fa— I mean, I'll have you down in a minute."

"GENTLY!" I was still scared, but not too scared to look out over Ernest Rausch's little farm. Behind the barn was a newer building—a large shed with a steel roof and several cables running into it. Brazie the bull had moved over by a stack of hay bales and was glaring up at me.

The drone began to descend.

"Billy."

"What?"

"Do you have this thing under control now?"

"Of course."

"I mean, *really* under control?" I was only about ten feet up, close enough to the ground that I figured I could survive a fall.

"I think so."

I would have preferred *Yes, absolutely, without question!*

"Can you make it go where you want now?"

The drone jerked to my left.

"Slowly!" I yelled. The drone slowed to a gentle walking pace. Billy guided it in a figure eight, lowered it a couple of feet, then raised it back up. It felt solid, not tippy at all. I got my knees up on the disk and arranged myself in a sitting, cross-legged position, but I didn't let go of the edges. It was a nice sensation, like riding a magic carpet. Billy sent me drifting along the outside of the fence, then back.

"Can you see through the phone camera?" I asked.

"Not very well. It's hanging kind of crooked."

"There's an odd-looking building behind the barn. Can you ease me over there so I can get a closer look?"

"You sure?"

I wasn't sure at all, but I said, "Yes."

"You're going to have to direct me. Once you're on the other side of the barn I won't be able to see you."

"Okay, but no more deadly heights, please. I don't want to go any higher than I am right now."

"Got it. Three meters maximum altitude. You ready?"

"Let's go."

The drone drifted toward the building. It was a peculiar sensation. The antigravity disk was completely silent and rock solid. I could lean to either side to look down, and the disk didn't tip at all. As I passed the barn, I caught a glimpse of several stainless steel cages through the window. The disk passed over the haystack. Brazie was on the other side, watching me. He seemed more puzzled than angry.

I was passing the corner of the barn when the drone stopped abruptly.

"Hey!" I yelled.

"Sorry. I can't see you anymore."

"Well don't jerk to a stop like that. I almost fell off!" I hadn't, really, but I wanted to make sure he was extra careful.

"Sorry. Now what?"

"Forward about thirty feet." The drone eased forward, and the mystery building came into view.

"Stop," I said. The disk eased to a complete stop. The mystery shed had white-painted metal sides and two windows with metal grates. Several electrical lines and coax cables fed into one end—a lot more than you'd expect from an outbuilding on a farm.

"Bring me forward and to the left, another thirty feet," I said. The drone moved off to the right. "I said left!"

"I can't see which way you're facing," Billy said.

"Go the opposite way you just did!"

"Okay, okay!"

The drone reversed course, taking me over an oblong cattle tank filled with greenish water and straight toward the back wall of the barn.

"Stop!" I yelled.

The drone stopped, and it wasn't a nice easy stop. I'd made the mistake of letting go of the disk, and I tumbled off.

22

Brazie

Ten feet doesn't seem like that far. It's only the height of a basketball hoop. But falling that far and landing flat on your back . . . try it sometime. For a more complete experience, do it over a neglected cattle tank.

I suppose landing in a tank full of slimy green water is better than landing on concrete or a bed of nails. Still, it was not an enjoyable experience. I came up spitting and coughing and yelling some words I refuse to repeat—at least not until the next time I get dumped in a tank full of scummy water.

The drone, meanwhile, was hovering ten feet over my head. My phone was dangling by a single strip of duct tape from its underside.

"You dumped me!" I yelled at the phone as I climbed dripping out of the tank.

"You yelled stop," Billy's voice was tinny and distant; I could hardly hear him.

"Get down here!"

"Straight down?"

"Yes! No! A little to the left!"

"Which way's left?" The drone edged toward the barn.

"No! The other way!"

The drone reversed course.

"That's good. Now straight down!" I raked a glob of green scum from my hair as, slowly, the drone began to descend. It was only a couple of feet above my head when I heard a snort. I turned around.

Brazie the bull was standing by the corner of the barn. He took a step toward me.

"No, Brazie," I said. "Stop."

"Stop?" Billy's voice said. The drone froze just out of my reach.

"Not the drone! The bull!"

Brazie snorted again. He shook his enormous head and stamped one front hoof.

I like my red hair. I figure it makes me special, because only about 2 percent of humans are blessed with the gene for red hair. But if there is one time when red hair is the last thing you want, it's when facing an irritable two-thousand-pound bull.

I was sure my hair looked to him like a

matador's cape. A wet, scummy red cape.

"It's just hair, Brazie." I took a step back. Brazie pawed the ground and lowered his head so his horns were pointing straight at me.

I said, "Billy, move the drone down a few feet and away from the barn." If I could get Brazie focused on the drone I might have time to get away.

The drone descended to head height and floated off to the left. Brazie ignored it. His shoulder muscles bunched. He lowered his hindquarters a few inches and launched himself at me.

What I should have done was jump back into the cattle tank, but it is difficult to think clearly when being charged by a bull. Actually, I don't think I was thinking at all. I just screamed and ran, with Brazie on my heels. I was about two seconds from being gored and trampled when something white charged around the far corner of the barn, legs and tongue flying, kicking up a cloud of dust as it came at me like an out-of-control semi. *A miniature white bull,* I thought in my panicky, confused state. *I'm about to become a bull sandwich!*

The small white bull barked and leaped. It was no bull—it was Gertrude! I threw myself to the side as Gertrude flew over me and clamped her teeth onto one of Brazie's ears. Brazie skidded to a stop and shook his head furiously, trying to dislodge the dog. He spun around in a circle, making a sound like a squeal inside a roar, but Gertrude would not let go. I knew I should run for safety, but seeing that dog hanging on by its jaws and being thrashed back and forth made me too mad to run. I spotted a pail next to the cattle tank. I grabbed it, scooped up a bucketful of scummy water, and ran at the crazed bovine, screeching like a banshee. Whatever a banshee is.

My yelling didn't distract Brazie, but the gallon of water certainly did. It hit him full in the face. He unleashed a bellow and jerked his head up with such force that Gertrude lost her grip and went flying into the air. Brazie, snorting and shaking his head, took off.

I looked around for Gertrude, expecting to find her lying broken on the ground. Instead, I found her paddling in circles in the cattle tank.

"Come on, girl," I said, leaning over the side of the tank. I helped her get her paws up over the lip of the tank, then reached over and wrapped my arms around her belly and lifted her out. Gertrude plopped wetly onto the ground.

"Are you okay?" I asked.

Gertrude shook, sending a mist of water and scum in every direction, but mostly at me. I backed away, sputtering. She seemed to be uninjured, judging from the ferocity of the tail wagging. She fixed her eyes on me and barked proudly.

"Good girl," I said.

Apparently I had issued an invitation. She came at me, tongue lolling, smiling that bulldog smile.

"Gertrude! No!" I shouted. "Down!" It didn't work. She weighed only a quarter as much as I do, but she made contact full on, paws hitting my belly and knocking me flat on my back. After that it was all dog breath, wet tongue, and tank scum. No dog has ever been happier to see anyone than Gertrude was to see me. And we hardly knew each other.

23

The Laboratory

"Gertrude, off!" I yelled. I shoved her wrinkly face aside and managed to get back on my feet. She looked up at me, wagging her tail so hard I was afraid it would fly off.

"Sit!" I said.

Gertrude sat, staring at me with those big brown eyes. I don't love animals as passionately as Myke Duchakis, but I can tell when they love me, and this dog had decided I was her soul mate.

"Are you okay?" Billy asked in a tinny voice. I had almost forgotten about the drone floating just over my head.

"I'm fine," I said. "No thanks to you!"

"What happened?" Billy asked.

"I almost got gored by Brazie!" I said. "Gertrude saved me."

"I *thought* I heard barking. You better get

back on the drone. I'll get you out of there."

Gertrude was gazing at me with unfiltered adoration.

"Do you think it can lift both me and Gertrude?"

"I doubt it. It won't lift me, and I only weigh twenty pounds more than you."

"We'll have to let her out through the gate, then."

"Why? We didn't come here to steal a dog."

"She *loves* me."

"Dogs love everybody. That's what dogs *do*!"

"Hang on a minute." I reached up to the drone and retaped my phone so the camera faced the metal lab building. "You see the building?"

"Yes."

"Good. I'm going to take a look inside. Keep an eye out."

The disk rose to head height.

"You wait here," I said to Gertrude. "I'll be back in a few minutes."

Gertrude stared at me, whining. "Stay," I said.

"I am not a dog!" Billy said.

"I wasn't talking to you," I said, even though I had been, really. I walked up to the door. The drone followed me. I twisted the doorknob.

"It's locked," I said.

"What kind of lock?"

"There's a keypad."

"Just a second . . . Hey, did you know Rausch has a Facebook page?"

"I'm not surprised. He's *old*."

"Try this." Billy rattled off a list of numbers. I punched them into the keypad. A green light came on. I tried the door again. This time it opened.

"How did you do that?" I asked.

"It's his birthday. Amazing how often that works. And that people put their birthdays on Facebook."

I stepped inside the building. The lights flickered on automatically.

"Hello," said a voice.

My heart stopped. I looked around to see who had spoken, but there was no one there.

"Hello?" I squeaked. One wall of the room was lined with cages. A long workbench covered with cables, printed-circuit boards, tools, and various unidentifiable devices ran along the opposite wall. There were two computer displays and a complicated-looking chair. Mounted above the chair's back was a thing that looked like a bicycle helmet with a bunch of wires coming out of it. Equally scary were the heavy Velcro straps attached to the arms. It looked like an electric chair, or some sort of torture device.

I heard the voice again.

"Give me food." It was coming from one of the cages. I could see now that four of the cages had occupants: a cat, a cocker spaniel, a Yorkshire terrier, and in the large cage at the end, a goat.

"I like cookies," said the goat.

The goat was wearing a collar.

I had seen collars like that before.

24

Client Key

A couple of months ago, Billy, Gilly, Myke Duchakis, and I had successfully shut down Area 51, the ACPOD animal-cybernetics program. Area 51 had been created without Gilly's knowledge, and it was horrible. The scientists behind it were performing surgeries on animals and implanting sensors in their brains. They had built a device that translated animal thoughts into human speech. It had seemed like a cool idea at first, but dozens of dogs, cats, and monkeys had been killed in the course of their research, and the animals that didn't die were miserable prisoners with wires sticking out of their heads and strange voices coming from collars around their necks.

Mostly what the animals said was "I like you," "I hate you," and "Feed me."

Like most cruel and unusual scientific

experiments, the original intent of the Area 51 program was noble. The researchers were hoping that eventually they would be able to use the technology to help people who had lost the power of speech— people who had suffered strokes, or who were in a coma. Ultimately, they hoped, the tech could be reverse engineered to allow humans to communicate directly with machines, and vice versa. Unfortunately, the animals suffered, and when Gilly found out about it, he shut the program down, freed the research animals from the various machines, and turned Area 51 into Clawz-n-Pawz, the animal adoption agency where Myke Duchakis works.[7]

Ernest Rausch had worked in Area 51, and it seemed that not all the lab animals had been freed.

"Hello, Mr. Goat," I said.

"*I like you,*" said the goat through the speaker on his collar. "*I would like a cookie.*"

"Sorry, I have no cookies."

"*I hate you,*" said the goat.

"*Let me go,*" said the cat. "*Let me go. Let me go.*"

"Fine, I'll let you all out, but let me do a little snooping first." I looked in on each of the animals. Only the goat and the cat were wearing collars; the dogs appeared to be unmodified.

"*Let me go,*" said the cat.

---

7 The whole sordid tale can be found in—you guessed it—*The Flinkwater Factor.*

The Yorkie started barking; the spaniel whined. I didn't need a translator to know that they were echoing the cat's request.

"Quiet!" I said sternly.

The dogs fell silent, but the cat continued its refrain: *"Let me out. Let me out. Let me out."* The goat was muttering its own mantra: *"I hate you. I hate you. I hate you."*

"Okay, whatever. Just wait a few minutes." I turned my attention to the computers. The first one demanded a password when I woke it up. I typed in Rausch's birthday.

PASSWORD INCORRECT

I tried a few other common passwords, including 123456, QWERTY, and PASSWORD. After five tries the screen displayed the message LOCKED OUT: TRY AGAIN IN AN HOUR. I woke the second computer and was greeted with the word "REMEMBER" emblazoned across the screen in Comic Sans. Once again, I was asked for a password.

"Let me go," said the cat.

I typed in LETMEGO. No luck.

"I hate you," said the goat.

I typed in IHATEYOU.

Ka-ching! A list of files appeared on the screen.

I scrolled through. Most of the file names were non-sensical, like d9389(Y88v3) or OXOGLETE. But a few looked promising:

Client Key
REMEMBER log
To Do List

I clicked on the "Client Key" file. A spreadsheet filled the screen.

10-1	G.B.	Partial restore	Canis lupus familiaris 02
9-30	W.B.	History, American	Canis lupus familiaris 02
9-29	G.B.	Code, AG-3601	Capra aegagrus hircus 01
9-27	R.C.	Evangeline	Felis catus 01
9-20	H.M.	Code, DB-1923	Felis catus 02
9-19	W.O.	Mathematical functions	Felis catus 02
9-16	G.B.	Code, AG-3601	Canis lupus familiaris 01
9-14	D.T.	King James	Felis catus 01
9-22	X.Z.	CRC Handbook	Canis lupus familiaris 01
7-19	M.T.	King James	Bos taurus 01
7-12	V.T.	King James	Bos taurus 01

It looked like a jumble of nonsense at first, but after a few seconds something jumped out at me.

Evangeline. My dad had told me that Ernest Rausch had helped him memorize that entire poem.

And just to the left of that were my dad's initials, R.C. And the number to the left of that looked like a date—September 27! That was the day my dad had memorized "Evangeline"!

I looked at the other initials and dates. G.B. had to stand for Gilbert Bates, and "Partial restore" probably meant that Rausch had restored some of Gilly's memories just this morning. His initials appeared in two other spots, followed by "Code, AG-3601." Hadn't Gilly said something about Rausch helping him remember code for his anti-gravity project?

The initials W.B. would be William Bates, and yesterday Billy had had his head stuffed with American history. Reading down the list, I noticed the initials X.Z. There couldn't be a lot of people with those initials, but I happened to know one: Xavier Zlotnick was the director of ACPOD's nano-technology program. I guessed that the other initials were also ACPOD employees.

The Latin-looking words on the right looked vaguely familiar, but I couldn't figure out why.

"*Let me go,*" said the cat.

"I'll let you out, but let me finish this, okay?"

The spaniel growled. The Yorkie snarled.

"*I hate you,*" said the goat.

"*I hate you,*" said the cat.

"What is *wrong* with you guys?" I glanced over

my shoulder at the cages. But the animals hadn't been talking to me. Their attention was on the door. I swiveled around in the chair to see what they were looking at and was hit with a clovey, nose-pinching wave of Bay Rum aftershave.

"Ginger Crump," said Mr. Rausch from the doorway. "Whatever are you doing here?"

25

Projac

The first time I met Ernest Rausch he hadn't seemed scary, just weird. I had almost felt sorry for him, even though he had been rude and dismissive. I figured he was one of those guys who had never got a date in high school, so he avenged himself on the world by acting all snooty and superior. There are a lot of guys like that working at ACPOD.

But here in his lab, caught red-handed snooping through his computer, I found his gangly, spiderlike body and his pointy goatee plenty scary.

He closed the door and shot the dead bolt.

"Oh!" I said.

"Oh?" he replied.

"I mean . . . " I stood up. "I was just leaving."

He closed the door. "But you just got here!"

"That's okay. I have to go. Somebody's

waiting for me." I took a tentative step toward the door. He did not step aside.

"I see you've met my friends," he said.

"*I hate you,*" the cat said, then followed it up with a hiss.

"Not very friendly friends," I said.

Rausch smiled. It was not a nice smile, more of a *gotcha* smirk.

"Ms. Crump, I do not usually accept walk-in clients, but for you I will make an exception."

"Um . . . I don't think I'm actually a client." I did *not* want to be included in his Client Key file folder. What I wanted was to get OUT. Like, NOW! Where was Billy? Where was the AG-3601? Where was *Gertrude*?

"Of course you are," Rausch said. "Your father is a big fan of my REMEMBER system."

"I don't know if 'fan' is the right word," I said.

"Everybody loves REMEMBER! Why, your friend Billy has the entire text of *A Comprehensive History of the United States* stored in his head. He can name every vice president, the names of their wives and children, and the names of their pets!" He spread his arms triumphantly. "How wonderful is that?"

"I see what you mean," I said, by which I meant, *I see that you are completely insane.*

"What would *you* like to know, Ginger?"

"Um . . . I would like to go now," I said.

"Don't be ridiculous. Think of this as an opportunity! Why, for you, I'm willing to waive my usual fee."

"Look, I'm sorry I came in here without permission. I won't say anything to anybody."

"Say anything? To whom? About what? I have no secrets."

"What about them?" I pointed at the cages.

"My pets? I am breaking no laws."

"*I hate you,*" said the cat.

"You're stealing people's memories."

"Not true! I am bestowing the gift of memories. *Useful* memories. Why should you clutter your mind with what you had for breakfast this morning when you could be enjoying the knowledge of the ages?"

"I'm leaving now," I said.

"I'm afraid that won't be possible." He set his bag on the floor and opened it to reveal a gray plastic cube about the size of a four-slice toaster. "Not until I demonstrate REMEMBER."

I made a dash for the door. Rausch shot out a long arm and snagged me as I tried to pass. I twisted out of his grasp and was fumbling with the dead bolt when he pulled a small object from his pocket and pointed it at me. I had about a tenth of a second to recognize the Projac before he pressed the trigger. The Projac made a *ghaaak* sound, and that's the last thing I remembered.

26

REMEMBER

I don't know how long I was knocked out, but when I came to, I was strapped into the complicated-looking chair. Rausch was sitting in front of me stroking his bolo tie with one hand while holding the Projac in the other.

"You're not supposed to have that," I said thickly. The pocket-model Projac he held could knock out an attacker from twenty feet away. A military-grade Projac could kill. Either way, the device was supposed to be top secret—nobody outside the ACPOD laboratory where it was being developed was supposed to know about it. I happened to know what it was because of the events last summer.[8]

"You stole a Projac from ACPOD," I mumbled. I was still pretty fuzzy after getting zapped.

---

8 You could read about it in . . . oh, never mind.

"I stole nothing. ACPOD stole from me. All my ideas, my brilliant innovations, my best ideas. The cybernetic interface that allows these animals to communicate with us was my idea. Gilbert Bates took my research and axed the project. But he won't steal REMEMBER, because he won't remember that REMEMBER exists. Is that not beautiful? I am using a machine that creates memories to eliminate all memories of the machine itself." He gestured at the REMEMBER machine. Several cables led from the device to the headset above me.

"Let me go," I said.

"Let me go," said the cat.

"I *will* let you go," Rausch said. "But first . . . what would you like to remember?" He set the Projac on his workbench and woke up one of the computers. "I have quite a selection here. *War and Peace*? That might be useful if you go to college. Or maybe you'd prefer a textbook? Biology, perhaps. Or a history of Western Europe?"

While he wasn't looking at me, I tested the straps gripping my forearms. They were tight, but I could twist my arms a little. The left strap was looser. With enough time I might be able to pull my hand through it.

"Why not just download the entire Library of Congress into my head while you're at it?"

"I cannot recommend that," Rausch said. "You

might forget your own name, and that would result in too many awkward questions. The more memories I load, the more you forget."

"Why are you doing this?" I figured the longer I could keep him talking, the better my chances of being rescued. Billy was out there someplace, and he must have seen Rausch arrive. Rausch hadn't said anything about the drone, so Billy must have kept it out of sight. What would he do? Contact his dad? The police? That would be the smart thing to do, but knowing Billy, he probably would try to rescue me himself.

"Why am I doing this?" Rausch chuckled in a not nice way. "Why does the sun rise? Because it must. And why should I not receive credit for my accomplishments?"

"But what are you going to do? I mean, your machine isn't much good if people have to forget as much stuff as they remember."

"That is where you are wrong! Forgetting is underrated. You must have seen things or done things that you would just as soon forget, yes?"

I thought for a moment. There were a few things, like the time I threw up on Danton Wills in biology class, and the time I accidentally killed my goldfish by giving him too much fish food—or maybe it was the gummy worms. But I wasn't going to admit that to Rausch.

"I like *all* my memories," I said.

"In any case, you don't get to choose. Your new memories will simply replace whatever you were thinking in the hours before downloading the new memories. The more complex and lengthy the introduced memories, the more you forget. If I were to give you, say, *War and Peace*, you would forget this conversation, and whatever you are thinking about right now, and probably everything you experienced or thought for the past twelve hours. But if I downloaded, as you suggested, the Library of Congress, you might forget how to breathe."

"That seems kind of random," I said.

"I'm still working on selective memory extraction. Such a technology would be tremendously useful. For example, if a man commits armed robbery, instead of sending him to prison, one could simply erase his memory of having committed the crime. There would then be no need to punish him. It would be as though he had never done it."

"The people who got robbed might disagree."

Rausch shrugged. "They remain robbed, but the person who did the robbing becomes innocent."

"That doesn't seem exactly fair."

"I'm sure such minor details will iron themselves out. In the meantime, have you decided what you want to remember?"

"I'm thinking about it." I looked at the machine.

"Obviously this is a brilliant, amazing, innovative, and incredibly valuable invention—"

"Thank you." He smiled a real smile. "I am, as you may have noticed, rather proud of it."

"I hadn't noticed—you seem so modest." Was I laying it on too thick?

"I try not to be too boastful," he said. Was he *blushing*?

"How does your machine work?" I asked.

"Ho-ho, wouldn't you and everyone else like to know!"

"I *would* like to know," I said. "I mean, since you're going to wipe my memory of today anyway, it won't matter if you tell me, right?"

"True," he said, stroking his wispy, almost invisible goatee and looking lovingly at his REMEMBER machine. I looked past him out the window. A familiar dark shape rose into view, with my cell dangling from its underside by a scrap of tape.

27

The Rauschinator

"REMEMBER works by altering existing memory engrams," Rausch said. "New information is implanted by flooding your brain with packets of trinary infocicles."

"Is 'infocicle' really a word?" I asked.

"I made it up," he said proudly. "REMEMBER is so revolutionary it demands a whole new language. For example, the altered engrams are known as rauschions, and the memory insertion process is called rauschination, and the headset above you is the Rauschinator."

"It looks like a bike helmet."

"It was once a bicycle helmet," he said. "Now it is a Rauschinator."

"That's brilliant," I said. "Tell me more!" The drone was still hovering outside the window. I wondered how much Billy could see with that cell phone camera. Could he tell I was strapped to a chair?

"Why not? You will forget your visit here, which will be very convenient for both of us. As I mentioned before, the system targets your most recently formed engrams."

"Then how come Billy forgot *me*?" I blurted. "You loaded him up with all the American history, and he forgot I even exist!"

Rausch stroked his goatee. "That is interesting. Does he not remember you at all?"

"No."

"In addition to recently formed engrams, REMEMBER targets extremely active engrams. He must have been thinking about you intently for those memories to have been overwritten."

"He was thinking about *me*?" I said. I have to admit, that gave me a romantic sort of buzz—right down to my toes. My eyes flicked to the window; the drone was gone.

"Apparently. Was he in love with you?" Rausch asked.

I wanted to shout, *HE'S STILL IN LOVE WITH ME!* But I forced myself to remain outwardly calm and said, "So are his deleted memories just . . . *gone*?"

Rausch smirked. "I am not a monster. Billy Bates's memories are secure."

"Then where are they?"

"You will soon find out." He turned back to his computer and scrolled through a long list of files. "I have *War and Peace, Moby-Dick, An Introduction to Quantum Physics* . . . "

"What about *Charlotte's Web*?" I almost had my left arm free.

"I'm afraid that file is not large enough for our purposes."

"I saw your client key," I said. "Are those all the people whose memories you changed?"

"Yes. Mostly ACPOD employees who were becoming too familiar with my work."

He stood and made an adjustment to the Rauschinator above my head. "I should probably shave your head for best contact—"

"No!" I shouted.

"Relax," Rausch said. "It is not essential, and we wouldn't want anyone to wonder what happened to that orange mop you call hair."

"It's not *orange*; it's almost-but-not-quite red. And it's not a mop."

"In any case, it will present no difficulties. The system has several layers of redundancies." He lowered the Rauschinator onto my head. I felt several sharp, cold pricks. I looked frantically at the window, hoping to see Billy's face, or even better, a SWAT team. But there was only blue sky. I did, however, hear something scratching at the door—probably Gertrude.

"Since you have expressed no preference, I think I will gift you with the entire text of *The Iliad*, in both the original Homeric Greek and the Fitzgerald translation."

"Wait!" I had no idea what I was going to say next. All I could think about was the Velcro straps holding me to the chair.

"Yes?"

"Did you know that Velcro was invented by a dog?"

That got his attention.

I said, "This guy was walking with his dog, and the dog got into some burdock—you know what burdock is? Those burrs that stick to anything?"

"Of course I know what burdock is!" Rausch said.

"Yeah, so the guy was looking at all the burdock stuck to his dog, and he saw that they were covered with these tiny hooks, like thousands of tiny flexible fishhooks. And he thought maybe he could make artificial burrs that would stick to artificial fur."

"Then it wasn't the dog who invented Velcro, it was the man."

"The dog brought it to his attention. You should never underestimate a dog. Your dog Gertrude, for example, is quite intelligent. I can hear her outside the door right now, scratching to get in."

"All in good time," Rausch said. "Pay no attention."

"You want to know something else about Velcro?"

"What?" Rausch snapped. He was getting irritated by my delaying tactics.

"Each little plastic hook on its own is weak. It's only because there are so many of them that it holds. Each little hook is like a—what did you call it? *Engram*. Like each engram is nothing by itself, but a bunch of engrams together makes a memory, right? So if you lose a few engrams, the memory gets fuzzy, but you don't forget it completely until you lose them all."

"Simplistic and crude," he said, "but somewhat correct." The scratching at the door was getting more frantic.

"Gertrude *really* wants to get in," I said.

"She can wait. We won't be long. Now, you have one more decision to make. Goat, or Yorkshire terrier?"

"You're going to give me a pet?" I said, confused.

"Certainly not! I'm asking you to choose a receptacle for your memories."

I didn't understand—and then suddenly I did.

28

Velcro

"You put the deleted memories in animal brains?"

"Precisely. Digital media does not work—I have tried it. But the higher mammalian brain is sufficient to hold several months worth of fresh engrams. These four creatures all have excess space in their craniums—more than enough space for your trivial memories."

I was rendered momentarily speechless. For a few seconds the only sound was that of Gertrude clawing at the door.

"What about Gertrude?" I said, hoping to buy more time. "She seems to want to come in."

"It's getting close to feeding time," Rausch said. "But never mind that. Now choose. Goat, or Yorkie?"

That gave me an idea. "Dog food!" I yelled. "Cat food! Goat food! Treats! Din-din!"

The goat unleashed an ear shattering bleat. *"Feed me!"* it said.

"Food," said the cat. *"Food! Food!"*

The spaniel whined. The goat bleated. Gertrude took her scratching up a notch. The Yorkie began barking frantically.

"Now see what you've done!" Rausch said.

"Sorry," I said. "I just love watching animals eat." The goat was butting its head against the front of its cage, and the spaniel had begun to howl.

"All right! Settle down! I'll feed you!"

That only intensified the cacophony. Rausch glared at me. "I should download the entire Internet into your meddling brain and funnel your memories into a rat!" He got up and began to feed the animals. I couldn't turn my head, but I heard the rattle of food pellets falling into a metal tray. The goat stopped bleating; the dogs and the cat increased their demands. I used the distraction to work on the straps. The Velcro was loosening one little hook at a time. Unfortunately, there were thousands of them. I could almost pull my left hand free.

Rausch fed the two dogs next. That really irritated the cat because, as all cats know, you always feed the cat first. *"FOOD! FOOD! FOOD!"* The little speaker on the cat's collar sounded as if it was about to blow.

My hand popped free. I reached over and tore

open the strap holding my other arm. My plan—I always have a plan—was to grab Rausch's Projac off the bench and zap him. It was a good plan, but I'd forgotten about the headset clamped to my skull. I tried to lift it off, but it was firmly attached with dozens of small, sharp points digging into my scalp. I was feeling around for some sort of release button or lever when Rausch grabbed my hands and pulled them away.

"What do you think you're doing?" he shouted in my face.

"FOOD!" the cat demanded.

I kicked him. It was a good hard kick, but it glanced off his hip. He forced my arms down, reattached the straps, stepped back out of range of my feet, and grabbed the Projac.

"Silly girl. What did you hope to accomplish?"

I stared back at him, angry, defeated, and out of ideas.

Someone knocked on the door. It wasn't a normal knock, but more like *thump . . . thump . . . thump*.

"Help!" I screamed. "HELP!" I screamed louder.

Rausch went to look out the window. "What the—"

The metal door exploded inward, followed by a flying black disk, then a white bulldog. The drone hit the far wall and fell to the floor. Gertrude took one look at me, bellowed, and leaped.

She wasn't aimed at me. The bulldog sailed past me and hit Rausch in the chest. The Projac went flying. I was straining desperately against the straps—they weren't as tight as before, but I couldn't quite get a hand free, and I couldn't see what was going on behind me. Rausch was yelling, Gertrude was snarling and barking, the cat was still demanding food, and the goat was bleating in a panicky sort of way. The drone seemed to be dead—crashing through the door must have been too much for it.

Where was Billy? I pulled against the straps with all my strength and felt the right one loosen. A second later I got both hands free and went to work on the headset. I heard a renewed bout of snarling from Gertrude. My hand found a small lever on one side of the headset; I pushed it and the helmet loosened. I slid out of the chair and looked to see what was going on with Gertrude and Rausch.

Gertrude was winning. She had Rausch on the floor and was standing on his chest. Her bared teeth were inches from his throat. I grabbed the Projac from where it had fallen.

"Gertrude!" I shouted.

Gertrude looked back at me and wagged her tail.

"Here, girl," I said.

She gave Rausch one more close-range snarl and hopped off his chest.

"Good girl," I said. She trotted over to me, wagging her tail so hard I was afraid she'd dislocate a hip. Rausch, looking both relieved and terrified, sat up.

I aimed at his chest and fired. The Projac made a *ghaaak* sound, like a cat barfing. The invisible electrical charge sent Rausch into a limb-flailing spasm, then he lay still.

I shot him again, just to make sure he stayed zapped. I would have given him a third blast if Gertrude hadn't been trying to drown me in wet kisses.

"Enough! Down, girl!" Gertrude *really* liked me. "You want some dog food?" I asked her. Gertrude did not have a speech collar, but the answer was clearly yes.

"*FOOD!*" said the cat.

I fed them both—the cat first—then went to find Billy.

29

Up a Tree

A bright red ATV was parked right outside the door. Rausch's transportation, no doubt. My cell was lying on the ground—it had flown off when the drone smashed through the door. My phone had not survived the impact; I would have to rely on a low-tech form of long-distance communication.

"Billy!" I shouted.

I heard a faint reply from the other side of the barn.

"Come on, Gertrude," I said. We walked around the barn, keeping an eye out for Brazie. I wasn't *too* worried, because I had both Gertrude and the Projac for protection, but a two-thousand-pound bull should never be taken lightly. As we came around the corner, I saw Brazie standing under an apple tree next to the house, looking up. Billy was clinging to the branches above him.

"Are you all right?" I called.

"No! I'm stuck in a tree with a bull underneath me!"

Gertrude growled, preparing to defend me if necessary.

"Stay, Gertrude!"

The bulldog looked up at me with what I took to be an expression of thanks. Even a bulldog doesn't relish the prospect of attacking something fifty times its size.

I aimed the Projac at the bull, then hesitated. I wasn't sure what the Projac's range was, and the bull was a good fifty yards away. It might have no effect, or the beam might spread out so much it would knock Billy out of the tree.

"Watch out," Billy yelled. "He's in a really bad mood!"

I couldn't blame the poor bull. Having your ear practically torn off by a dog and getting a bucket of water up the nose would put anybody in a bad mood.

"Hey, Brazie!" I yelled.

Brazie's head swiveled in our direction. I waved my arms and jumped up and down. Brazie snorted, shook his head, and turned to face us. It occurred to me that the Projac might not be powerful enough to stop him. I might have to make a dash for the cattle tank. Brazie lowered his head so that his horns were pointing straight at me, and he charged.

You would think an animal as heavy as a car would take some time to accelerate. You would be wrong. I hardly had time to gasp in fear before he attained top speed, and his maximum velocity was a lot faster than I could run—the cattle tank was not an option.

I aimed the Projac and fired.

Ghaaak!

Brazie stumbled a little, but he didn't slow down much. Gertrude let out a bellow and launched herself at the bull.

Ghaaak!

The invisible beam hit both animals. Gertrude collapsed, but Brazie kept coming.

Ghaaak! Ghaaak! Ghaaak!

The fifth *ghaaak* did it. Brazie hit the dirt nose-first and skidded to an unconscious halt about six feet away from me. My heart was hammering so hard I could feel it in my bones. I ran over to Gertrude, who had narrowly missed getting trampled. She rolled her eyes and licked my hand, but she couldn't stand up.

"It's okay, Gertrude," I said. "You'll be fine in a few minutes."

Billy climbed down from the tree.

"Where'd you get the Projac?" he asked.

"I borrowed it from Mr. Rausch." I looked back at the lab building. "You won't even believe what he's been doing in there. He's been using animals to store people's memories."

"My lost memories are stuck in some animal?"

"Not *some* animal." I looked down at Gertrude. She had managed to roll onto her belly, but she still couldn't quite stand up. She gazed lovingly up at me and whined. "I think they're in *that* animal."

"Oh. I guess that's why Rausch brought her to my tutoring session."

"I think it must be why Gertrude attacked Brazie the first time. She was protecting me. She attacked Rausch, too." I jerked my thumb at Rausch's laboratory.

"Is he still in there?"

"Yeah, but he's sleeping." I held up the Projac. "I suppose we'd better call somebody before he wakes up."

"I already did," Billy said. "I called Gilly, and your dad, and the police, and the fire department."

"Why the fire department?"

"I called everybody I could think of." We could hear sirens in the distance.

"We should probably check on Rausch," I said. "Make sure he doesn't wake up."

Just as I said that I heard the whine of an engine starting. I ran around the corner of the barn in time to see Rausch on his ATV, speeding through the open gate.

30

Animals

After that things got confusing. The police, two fire trucks, Gilly, and my father arrived all at once, bringing with them a thousand questions. Billy and I both tried to explain what had happened. At first Gilly was upset about Billy hijacking and wrecking his AG-3601, but once he heard that Rausch had taken me prisoner, he had to admit that it had been necessary. My dad seemed mostly mad that we'd come out there on our own. The cops went chasing after Rausch. The firefighters ran around looking for fires and were disappointed not to find any. Right around then, Brazie woke up. He staggered to his feet and took off after the firefighters—I think he was offended by their bright yellow slickers. They scrambled up onto the fire truck. Brazie stamped and snorted and looked around for someone else to gore. The rest of us took refuge in the lab building, where Gilly immediately went to work on Rausch's computer.

"*I like you,*" said the goat, its eyes fixed on Gilly. "*Feed me!*"

"Do you think Gilly's memories are in that goat?" I whispered to Billy.

"I hope not. He's still getting over everybody thinking he was a Sasquatch."

Gilly said, "We have a problem. Rausch managed to delete several files from his servers."

"And he took his memory machine with him," I said.

"How big is this thing?" my dad asked.

"It's like a big toaster. And the thing he attaches to your head is a bike helmet with a bunch of wires."

"We'll get him," my dad said. "Is there anything else we should know?"

"There was a file called Client Key on his computer. Is that still there?"

"I don't see it," Gilly said. "Why?"

"I looked at it before Rausch caught me snooping. It was a list of people he had rauschinated."

"Rauschinated?"

"That's what he calls what he does. He calls the bike helmet thing a Rauschinator. He fills up people's heads with books and then sticks their memories in animals. There were a bunch of initials on the list I saw, including yours and Billy's."

I looked at my dad. "Yours too. And after each one were some Latin words and some numbers. Like for Billy it was . . . " I closed my eyes and tried to remember. "I think it was *Canis lupus familiaris* zero two."

Billy said, "Isn't *Canis lupus familiaris* the Latin name for a dog?"

"That's right," Gilly said. "I'll bet the number identifies the specific dog."

"It's Gertrude," I said. "Gertrude was with Rausch when he came over to your house and . . . well . . . Gertrude really likes me." I might have been blushing. I looked at Billy. He was blushing too.

"I hate you," said the cat.

"All of them have collars with tags," my dad said. He was over by the cages looking at the animals. "The cocker spaniel is number three, the Yorkie is number one, and the cat . . . "

The cat hissed and backed into the corner of its cage. *"I hate you."*

"I can't read the cat's collar, and I'm not sticking my hand in there. The goat's tag says oh one. Ginger, do you remember any more of the list you saw?"

"I saw the initials X.Z., so I suppose that's Mr. Zlotnick. And it said what memories were downloaded—American history for Billy, 'Evangeline' for you, and some drone code for

Gilly. I don't remember the rest. A few of them had something about a king. I wonder where the rest of the animals are."

"Has anyone looked in the barn?" my dad said. He looked out the door. "I'd check, but I'm not sure I'm fast enough to outrun that bull."

"You're not," I said. "But you could use this." I pulled the Projac from my pocket and handed it to him.

His mouth fell open. "Where did you get this?"

"From Mr. Rausch."

My dad looked at Gilly. "This is the missing prototype."

"It takes five shots to knock out Brazie," I said.

"You used this on the bull?"

"I used it on Mr. Rausch, too," I said proudly. "Only he didn't stay down long."

My dad gave me the Look. "Ginger, you cannot go around shooting people with an experimental weapon. You might have killed him!"

"He started it," I said.

Dad pocketed the Projac and said, "Be that as it may . . . " It was one of those things he said when he didn't know what to say. He went to the door and looked outside.

"If we don't do something about Brazie, we'll be stuck here forever," I said.

"One of the fire crew has managed to get into

the cab," he said. "They're driving through the main gate . . . they're on the road now, and the bull is chasing them."

I ran to the door and looked out in time to see the fire truck—and Brazie—disappearing into the sunset.

31

Macaroni and Cheese

My dad and I left Billy and Gilly to salvage what they could from Rausch's computer and went over to the barn. We were greeted by a horse, two cows, and a monkey. The horse and cows were confined to their stalls; the monkey was dangling from a miniature trapeze inside a cage. They all had something to say—not in human language, but in neighs, moos, and screechy gibbering—and they were all wearing collars with numbered tags.

"It must be feeding time," I said.

We gave the cows and the horse some hay and alfalfa. I found a burlap bag full of peanuts and some overripe bananas in a cabinet near the monkey's cage. He seemed to like them.

"You said there were about ten names on the list?" my dad said.

"At least."

"Then we're still missing some animals."

"Even if we find them all, it won't do us any good," I said. "Unless we can figure out how to get the memories out of the animal and back into the person's brain. And we don't know which animal has whose memories."

"We will," my dad said. "But right now we should go home, eat dinner, and have a talk about your reckless and irresponsible behavior."

I looked at him with shock. "If it weren't for me, you wouldn't even know what Rausch has been doing!"

"That doesn't excuse the fact that you put yourself and Billy in extreme danger."

"But what about Mr. Rausch? He's still free! And Brazie is running around someplace, and you don't even remember our own cat, and who knows what else? And what about the animals? Who's going to take care of them?"

"I'll have a couple of my security guys stay here in case Rausch comes back. They'll make sure the animals are taken care of. As for the rest of it, it's been a long day. We'll deal with it tomorrow."

Gilly and Billy were trying to fit Rausch's computers, Billy's WheelBot, and the damaged drone into Gilly's SUV. Gertrude came bounding up to me and went into her licking routine.

"I'm taking everything to ACPOD," Gilly said. "There are still traces of the deleted files here. I'll put our techs on it."

"We're taking Gertrude, too," Billy said. "Unless you want her."

Gertrude looked at me and whined.

"I'd love to, but Barney might have a problem." I turned to Gilly. "I'm sorry your drone got wrecked," I said.

Gilly shrugged. "It was just a beta. I'm glad it served a useful purpose." He wedged the drone between the WheelBot and the computers, then shut the tailgate. "I hear you went for quite a ride. You know, the AG-3601 really wasn't designed for human transport."

"Believe me, it was not intentional."

Dad and I didn't talk much on the way home. I was buzzing inside, remembering the terrifying events of the past couple hours. I couldn't blame him for being mad. What Billy and I did was pretty crazy, and he was right—some really bad things could have happened. On the other hand, nobody else was doing anything about the missing memories, and Rausch was still out there with his REMEMBER machine. I kept thinking about Billy and Gertrude.

When we got home, Mom was waiting with an elaborate feast of microwaved macaroni and cheese and a salad mix from a bag—a typical Sunday dinner at the Crumps. Over dinner, Dad filled her in on the events of the afternoon. Every time he added another detail, she would shoot me her dagger eyes. You might think she'd be mad at Mr. Rausch instead of me, but that's because you don't know my mom. The rest of the meal was pretty much them trying to make me feel bad about being irresponsible.

Did I feel bad? Not really. But I knew better than to argue.

After they released me from their shaming session, I went to my room and checked my tab to see if *Charlotte's Web* had been magically restored. It had not. I thought about Dottie Tisk, probably curled up in her bed reading about Fern and Wilbur and Charlotte. Somehow I made it all Dottie's fault— not just Charlotte, but the whole memory-stealing thing, even though she had nothing to do with it. I guess in some ways I'm like my mom. I don't always get mad at the right person, as I was about to learn.

32

A Face at the Window

I thought I'd have trouble getting to sleep that night because my mind was going a thousand miles an hour. It's not every day you have to deal with an angry librarian, a flying disk, a raging bull, and a mad scientist trying to replace your memories with an ancient Greek poem. But I must have been pretty worn out, because I passed out right away after crawling into bed.

I didn't sleep long. I was awakened by a *tap-tap-tap* at my window. I tried to ignore it.

Tap-tap-tap. I looked at my clock—a few minutes after midnight. I sat up and looked at the window. A pale face stared back at me through the glass. *Tap-tap-tap.*

Ghost! I thought. That only lasted half a second, because I don't believe in ghosts. Usually. But my heart was pounding. I was about to scream for my parents . . . then I recognized the face.

It would have been easier to believe in a ghost. For one thing, my window was twelve feet above the ground, and for another thing, it was Dottie Tisk.

I jumped out of bed and went to the window. Dottie was clinging to the branches of the hackberry tree with one hand and knocking on the glass with her other. I opened the window.

"Hi," she said, as if this was the most ordinary of meetings.

"Hello," I replied, then waited to see what remarkable thing would happen next.

"Can I come in?" she said after an awkward silence. "I'm kind of losing my grip here."

"Clearly," I said. In my opinion, Dottie had lost her grip a long time ago. I helped her climb inside. "What are you doing here?" I asked unpolitely.

"I brought you this." She pulled a book from the waistband of her sweatpants.

Charlotte's Web!

I was gobsmacked.[9] After our last conversation I figured she'd burn that book before letting me anywhere near it.

"Uh . . . thank you," I said, taking the book from her.

"I know how hard it is to stop in the middle

---

9 I've been waiting my whole life to use that word.

of a good book," she said. "I just finished it an hour ago, and I couldn't sleep. But you have to give it back to me when you're done, because I want to read it again."

"It's that good?"

"I think it might be the best book ever."

I paged through the first couple of chapters. Everything seemed to be in order—Wilbur was still a pig, and Charlotte could talk. "You really didn't have to. I mean, it could have waited until tomorrow."

Dottie shook her head fiercely. "I might forget. I forget things a lot."

"You and a lot of other people."

"My mom says I have a mind like a sieve. I mean, I know I read that book once before, but I couldn't remember what happened in the end." She sat down on my bed. "It's strange, because some things I remember really well. I can remember all of Father's sermons, even the boring ones."

"Aren't sermons *supposed* to be boring?"

Dottie's eyes flashed. "Father can be quite compelling."

"I'm sure he can," I said.

Dottie sighed. "But mostly you're right. He just says the same things over and over, mostly Bible quotes, and I already know the Bible word for word." Dottie stared at the floor.

"Thank you for the book," I said.

Dottie nodded and stood up. "I should get back." She looked out the window at the hackberry tree. "Um, do you think I could use your door?"

"Sure, only we have to be quiet. My mom gets cranky if I wake her up."

We made it downstairs without incident, and I let her out the front door.

"Good night," I said. "I'll get the book back to you as soon as I'm done."

Dottie walked off down the sidewalk. I looked at the book in my hand, then went back to my room to read.

I finished reading *Charlotte's Web* at three a.m. Dottie was right. It was a really good book. I dreamed of pigs and spiders.

33

Spinning Disks

My mom woke me up.

"I know you had an eventful day yesterday," she said, "but this is ridiculous."

I squinted blearily at my clock.

"It's not even noon yet," I said. "No school today. Teachers' conferences, remember?"

She arched one perfect eyebrow and zeroed in on the book lying next to my pillow. "I see you found the book you were looking for."

"I borrowed it from Dottie Tisk. How come you're not at work?"

"I have been at work since seven o'clock this morning. I just came home to make sure you had emerged from your coma."

"I have emerged," I informed her.

"Emerge some more."

I sat up. "Is Dad home?"

"Your father is at work, trying to untangle the can of worms you and Billy Bates opened yesterday."

"Hey, I didn't put the worms in the can," I said.

"Be that as it may, he has requested your presence. He and Gilly are in the neuroprosthetics department working on Ernest Rausch's computer."

Dad had taken his WheelBot to work, so I had to walk. The ACPOD laboratories were a mile away, so I brought Charlotte along to keep me company. I don't know why, but I wanted to read the really sad part again. I read as I walked, and it was an unseasonably hot and humid day, and the sad part was really sad, so I arrived at the labs exuding fluids from my pores *and* my eyes. I know that sounds quite unattractive. It was.

"Are you okay?" asked Ms. Ketter, who was manning—or rather, womanning—the security desk.

"I'm fine," I said. I showed her the book. "I was just reading something sad."

"I read that book," Ms. Ketter said, smiling. "It's not sad in the end."

"I was rereading the sad part."

Ms. Ketter seemed to understand that. "Are you here to see your father?"

I nodded and stepped over to the scanner.

Since the events of last summer, ACPOD had upped its security systems. If you don't have an employee badge you have to go through all sorts of procedures—fingerprints and so forth. Even I, the daughter of Director of Cyber-Security Services Royce Crump, had to submit to a retina scan.

My retinas passed, even with the drying tears to obscure them.

I had never been in the neuroprosthetics lab before. It was surprisingly small, with a single workbench and only one computer terminal. Gilly, my dad, and Billy were sitting in front of the display. Gertrude was sleeping on a folded towel in the corner.

I watched Billy flip through screen after screen of what looked like gibberish.

"That doesn't look good," I observed.

My dad nodded. "It's not. Rausch erased most of his files and encrypted the rest. Our standard decryption programs aren't working."

"I'm running some nonstandard ones now," Billy said.

"We were hoping you could remember more of what you saw when you looked at his client key," Gilly said. "See if you can reproduce a line or two, character for character. That will give our pattern-recognition system something to key off of."

I wasn't sure I could do that, but I sat down at the keyboard and tried. I typed,

10-1 G.B.   Partial restoration   Canis lupus familiaris

It didn't look quite right. "I think there was a two-digit number after the Latin."

"Assuming that it identified a specific animal, that would make sense," Gilly said. "All the animals had numbers on their tags. Try zero one."

I did so. It still looked wrong. I tried the only other line I remembered.

9-27 R.C.   Evangeline   Felis catus 01

"I think that one's accurate," I said. I went back to the first line I'd typed. The word "restoration" looked wrong. I changed it to "restore." That looked better. "Is that enough?"

"You can't remember any more?" Billy said.

"Unlike *some* people, I do not have an eidetic memory," I said peevishly. "I know your initials were there, and probably the Latin name for dog, since we're pretty sure your memories got transferred to Gertrude."

Gertrude, hearing her name, emitted a sleepy bark from the corner.

"Okay, we'll go with what we've got," Billy

said, taking my place at the terminal. "If we can crack Rausch's encryption, we might be able to access all his records and figure out how to get our lost memories back." His fingers flew across the keyboard. "There."

"You got it?" I asked.

"Not yet. The pattern-recognition program is running. This might take a while."

The screen showed nothing but a spinning, multicolored disk, indicating that the computer was thinking.

"How long is a while?"

Billy shrugged. "A couple hours," he said.

I am not a girl who can sit staring at a computer for two hours. Besides, the neuroprosthetics lab smelled like three guys had been working there for hours, with the faint, lingering scent of Ernest Rausch's abominable cologne.

"Do you need me anymore?" I asked.

They ignored me. They were staring at the spinning disk like three hypnotized owls. I'd seen guys do that before, as if staring hard at the display could make the disk spin faster, while completely ignoring the female person in the room.

"What about Mr. Rausch? Have they found him yet?"

"The police are working on it, Ginger," my father said without looking at me.

"I'll just be going, then."

Nobody said anything.

"Maybe I'll rob the bank, or dance down the street in my underwear."

One of them grunted—I couldn't tell who. It might have been Gertrude.

34

Plan D

I stole my father's WheelBot. I knew the key code, and it was just sitting there in the ACPOD parking lot, and my dad was so absentminded he'd probably figure he'd gotten to work by some other means. Also, I was kind of irritated by the way he'd ignored me once I was no longer useful.

As I rolled down the street stewing about that, I decided to stew about some other people I was mad at. Like my mother, who wouldn't tell me why our town was called Flinkwater. And Mr. Rausch, who had erased me from my fiancé's memory. And Billy, for forgetting me, even if it wasn't his fault. And Dottie Tisk . . . except I wasn't mad at Dottie anymore since she had brought me the book.

That reminded me that I'd promised to get it back to her as soon as possible. I rolled left on

Third Street and aimed the WheelBot in the direction of the giant Jesus statue.

I knew Dottie wouldn't want her parents to see the book, so I parked the WheelBot two houses down, tucked Charlotte into my waistband, and pulled my T-shirt over it. My plan was to sneak around to Dottie's bedroom window and, if she was there, give it to her. My plan worked perfectly until I got to her window and peeked inside. Dottie wasn't there.

Okay, on to plan B. I went to the front door and rang the bell. Maybe Dottie would answer it, or maybe her mom would let me in and I could slip Dottie the book without Mrs. Tisk seeing.

No answer. They must all be at church doing churchy things. On to plan C.

I went back to Dottie's window. If I could open it, I could climb inside and hide the book under her mattress where she'd hidden it before.

The window was locked. I thought hard for a moment and came up with plan D. I would hide the book somewhere on their property and try to get a message to Dottie telling her where. I looked around for a protected place where it wouldn't get rained on or anything. The garage? I tried the garage door. Locked. Who locks their garage in Flinkwater? Hardly anybody even locks their front door. I peered through the grimy window. I couldn't see much, but what I did see made the hairs on the back of my neck stand up.

Parked inside was a bright red ATV. The only red ATV I knew of in Flinkwater was the one Ernest Rausch had escaped on yesterday. Why was it parked in the Tisks' garage?

I knew what I should do. I should call my dad. But I imagined how that might go.

"Dad, there's a red ATV parked in the Tisks' garage."

"That's nice, Ginger, but I'm watching this very important spinning disk right now."

"Dad, I think it's Mr. Rausch's ATV. I think the Tisks are harboring a fugitive!"

"Don't be ridiculous, Ginger. The Tisks are a fine, upstanding family, and I'm sure there are many red ATVs in Flinkwater County."

"But Dad—"

"Look, the disk is spinning faster!"

"But—"

"Ginger, please . . . "

I did not want to have that conversation. I was already mad at him, and I didn't want to get any madder. Also, my cell had died back at Rausch's farm, so I couldn't call him even if I wanted. Anyway, the next time I saw my dad I wanted to have some solid evidence that Rausch had been there. I went back to the house. The front and back doors were locked. I tested all the windows. Locked.

What would Billy do? I wondered. He would probably pick the door lock. I didn't have his lock-picking skills, but maybe the Tisks, being fanatical door lockers, had hidden a spare key someplace. I went back to the front and looked under the welcome mat. I turned over some rocks in the garden. I ran my fingers along the sill above the door. I reached into the mail slot and felt around. No key. I performed a similar search around the back door. Nada. I went back to the front and stood in the shadow of the Jesus statue and tried to imagine where I would hide a key.

"I'm out of ideas," I said to the statue. "Any suggestions?"

Jesus did not reply. I sat down on the concrete base of the statue, thinking hard. Maybe there was no hidden key, and I was wasting my time. I looked down at Jesus's feet. Some of the paint was peeling off. Idly, I picked at the loose paint with my fingernail, then felt bad about it. I don't object to a bit of minor vandalism—I'd TPed Myke Duchakis's house last Halloween—but I didn't think I should mess with Jesus's feet. I noticed, however, that there was a gap between his left foot and the concrete base, and an inch of string sticking out of it.

I pulled on the string and out came a key.

35

The Garage

The Tisks' house felt dead inside. The only sound was the hammering of my heart, and the only colors were beige, white, or gray. The furniture looked as if it had never been sat on or used. A sepia-toned print over the sofa showed Eve in the Garden of Eden being tempted by the serpent.

I crept down the hall and peeked into the first room. There were two beds, neatly made with coverlets the color of raw canvas. Mr. and Mrs. Tisk's room, I assumed.

The next room was Dottie's. I shoved Charlotte between her sheet and the mattress so she'd feel it when she climbed into bed.

There was one more bedroom at the end of the hall. The door was closed. I twisted the knob and eased the door open. One bed, with the covers thrown back and the sheets tangled, but it wasn't the bed that got my attention — it was the lingering aroma of Bay Rum aftershave.

As far as I was concerned that was proof that Ernest Rausch had stayed at the Tisks' last night. I checked under the bed and in the closet, hoping to find the REMEMBER machine, but there was nothing. Maybe it was in the garage with his ATV. I found a key hanging on the wall near the back door. The tag on the key said GARAGE. I let myself out, went back to the garage, and unlocked the side door and stepped inside.

The first thing I noticed was Dottie, sitting in a chair on the other side of the ATV, staring at me with a peculiar wide-eyed expression. Her hair looked weird — then I saw that it wasn't her hair; she was wearing the Rauschinator.

The second thing I noticed was the powerful smell of Bay Rum.

The door slammed behind me.

"Ms. Crump," said Ernest Rausch. "Shall we take up where we left off?"

I tried to run around him to the door. He spread his long arms and tried to grab me. I ducked under his left arm and got my hand on the doorknob, but Rausch grabbed the back of my belt and yanked me back. I twisted free and jumped onto the ATV. Rausch lunged for me, but I jumped back down on the far side of the ATV.

"You can't get out," he said, edging around the back of the ATV.

I waited for him to get almost all the way around, then jumped onto and over the ATV, heading for the door. He was too fast for me. I had to back off. Once again we faced each other across the ATV. I took a quick look at Dottie. The wires from the Rauschinator led to a square plastic box on the floor—the REMEMBER machine. Dottie was about to get rauschinated, if she hadn't been already. She looked scared.

"You okay?" I asked her, keeping an eye on Rausch.

Dottie shook her head. I noticed Mr. Peebles then, sitting calmly on the floor next to her feet.

"Dottie is about to memorize the Greek and Latin translations of the Old Testament," Rausch said. "To take her mind off that Duchakis boy."

"Myke?" I glanced back at Dottie.

"I wrote some things about him in my diary," she said. "My mom found it."

"You're in love with Myke Duchakis?" I said.

She was blushing. "She says I'm too young to have a boyfriend, so she told Uncle Ernie to give me another attitude adjustment."

"Uncle Ernie?" I said.

"That's right," Rausch said. "Mabel is my sister. This is a family affair, and you have rudely interrupted us." He shrugged. "But it doesn't matter. An hour from now you'll both have other things to think about."

"Do you *want* to forget Myke?" I asked Dottie.

"No," she said.

"I didn't think so."

I grabbed the Rauschinator and yanked it off Dottie's head. "Ow!" she cried out.

Rausch moved faster than I thought possible, leaping onto and over the ATV and diving at me. Before I could move, he crashed into us, knocking Dottie off the chair and landing on top of me. Mr. Peebles yowled and jumped onto a metal shelf against the back wall.

I kicked; I clawed; I bit. It didn't work. I tried to scream, but Rausch had me wrapped in his long, sinewy arms, squeezing so hard I could hardly breathe.

"If you don't stop, I'll squeeze until your ribs crack," he said. I stopped struggling. "Much better," he said, relaxing his grip slightly. "And congratulations—you've moved to the head of the line. Dottie will have to wait her turn, but she's a good girl." He raised his voice. "You're a good girl, aren't you, Dottie?"

The answer was a whining growl. Dottie was on the ATV, revving the engine.

"No!" Rausch yelled. Dottie twisted the accelerator; the machine leaped forward and hit the garage door. The plywood panels shattered; the ATV burst through onto the driveway and screeched onto the street.

Go, Dottie, I thought. *Go!*

36

Slapped

Dottie was free, but my situation had not improved. Rausch was furious. Holding me with one arm wrapped painfully around my waist, he grabbed the chair Dottie had been sitting in and dragged it over by the metal shelves, where it wasn't visible from the street. He slammed me into the chair.

"Do. Not. Move," he said. He backed away, keeping me in sight, and picked up the REMEMBER machine and the Rauschinator.

"Dottie will bring the police," I said hopefully.

Rausch laughed. "I think not. My niece is a good girl. She wouldn't want to get her parents in trouble."

"She just stole your ATV and crashed it through a closed garage door," I pointed out.

"True." A shadow of worry crossed his face, but he shrugged it off. "In any case, very soon now you will have nothing to tell. Hold still." He lowered the Rauschinator onto my head. I tried to kick him you-know-where, but he turned his hip and deflected my foot. Then he slapped me, hard, right across the face.

I don't know if you have ever been slapped hard in the face by a grown man, but if you ever are, you will find that it's not like the movies when people slap each other all the time and they're just, like, *ouch*. A real slap is much worse. My head snapped back, my ears were ringing, and everything went dim for a second. But what happened next was kind of cool.

My eyes regained focus, and I saw that Rausch's head had been replaced by a large fur ball. Furthermore, a large, puffed-up tail seemed to be jutting from the place where he usually kept his goatee, and the air was vibrating with a horrific high-pitched howling.

The howling wasn't me. It was the normally sedate Mr. Peebles, who had attached himself to Rausch's face. Rausch was howling too. I don't know which of them was louder. I'm sure it would have been Rausch if he hadn't been trying to scream through Mr. Peebles's furry body.

Mr. Peebles was hard at work, attempting to detach Rausch's ears with his unsheathed claws while biting the top of his head. I don't know how long it went on. Maybe only a few seconds, but to me—and probably to Mr. Rausch—it felt much longer. Mr. Peebles finally decided his job was done. He sprang from Rausch's face and landed next to me. Rausch was staggering around, disoriented and in obvious pain.

Mr. Peebles looked up at me and said, "Merp?"

"Merp," I replied.

"Aargh!" cried Mr. Rausch.

"Let's get out of here!" I said to Mr. Peebles.

We took off through the shattered garage door.

37

Rauschinated

Mr. Peebles refused to join me on the WheelBot. I felt bad about leaving him behind, but I had to get to a phone quick. Myke Duchakis lived just a few blocks away, so I headed over there. Guess what I saw parked in his driveway.

Yup, a red ATV.

I hit the doorbell about six times. Myke answered the door with his chinchilla perched on his shoulder.

"Did you call the police?" I said.

Myke and his chinchilla both looked surprised. I guess I was kind of frantic.

"Um . . . no? Why?"

"Gimme your cell."

Myke reached into his pocket and handed me his phone. As I punched in 911, I saw Dottie peeking around the corner.

"What's going on?" Myke asked.

"Ask your girlfriend."

"Girlfriend?" He looked back at Dottie, who ducked out of sight.

"Thanks a lot, Dottie," I yelled.

"Hello?" said the 911 operator. "Can I help you?"

"Yes!" I told her I'd been assaulted. She had a million questions. I tried to answer them, and finally she said she'd send a car over to the Tisks' house.

I disconnected and called my dad. He answered on the third ring.

"Ginger?" he said.

"Are you still at the lab?"

"Yes. We're making progress."

"I found Rausch." I quickly told him what had happened, and how Mr. Peebles had saved me. "I called the police, but Rausch might be gone by now." I heard a siren approaching.

"We'll get there as soon as possible," my dad said. "Stay where you are."

Stay where I was?

No way! I tossed the phone back to a very confused-looking Myke Duchakis and ran outside to the WheelBot. I arrived at the Tisks' moments after the police. The two cops were peering through the broken garage door with their guns drawn. I hopped off the unicycle and came up behind them.

"He's not moving," said one of the officers. He raised his voice. "Sir! Are you all right?"

"I'm going in." The cop ducked his head and entered the garage. A moment later he said, "Call an ambulance."

Right then my dad and two of his security guys pulled up in an ACPOD van. My dad jumped out, gave me the Look, and followed the cops into the garage. A minute later he came out, looking grim.

"Is he dead?" I asked. "Did Mr. Peebles kill him?"

He shook his head. "Didn't I tell you to stay at Myke's?"

"Sorry."

He put his hands on my shoulders and looked at my face. "Are you okay?" He touched my cheek where Rausch had slapped me.

"I think so. He hit me really hard, but it feels okay now."

"You're going to have a bruise."

"What happened to him?"

Dad shook his head. "He's sitting in there with that device on his head, looking very confused. He doesn't seem to know who he is, or where he is, or what is going on. He's quite agitated, talking a blue streak but not making any sense. He's talking about banana slug mating rituals and obscure baseball statistics and the history of sailing vessels and who wrote which Beatles songs and all sorts of other random trivia. It's as if somebody ripped the encyclopedia into a million pieces and shoved it into his brain."

"He rauschinated himself?"

"So it would seem."

38

Not Quite the End of the Story

They took Mr. Rausch to the hospital and put a guard outside his room, just in case he tried to escape. My dad took the REMEMBER machine to ACPOD, and maybe you think that's the end of the story, but you would be wrong.

A whole bunch of people—including Billy and my dad—were still missing huge chunks of their memories. And with Rausch in a coma, nobody knew how to get them back.

The Tisks returned home to find their house festooned in yellow police tape. They managed to convince the cops that they had had no idea that Mrs. Tisk's brother Ernest had been wanted by the police, and they said they were shocked—*shocked*—that he would subject their dear daughter Dottie to an experimental procedure. I was sure they were lying, but nobody was listening to me.

Dottie was still hiding out at Myke's, so far as I knew. Would *she* blow the whistle on her parents? I went back to Myke's house to ask her, but both Myke and Dottie had left.

"I don't know where they went," Mrs. Duchakis told me. "But they took a basket of kittens with them."

Where would Myke go with a basket of kittens?

I went over to Addy Gumm's. She answered her door holding two squirming kittens.

"Yes, dear, they were just here. I was only able to take these two—I already have eighteen cats, you see, and I promised the mayor to keep it down to twenty. Myke took the others to find them another home."

"Where?"

"I really don't know."

I texted Billy.

> Rausch has been rauschinated.
> Trying to find Dottie. Where are you?

I got a text back immediately.

> I'm at home. Dottie and Myke are here. Do you need another cat?

Dottie was at Billy's? I jumped on the WheelBot.

A few minutes later Alfred let me in. I noticed that the holes in the walls had been repaired, and there were no new ones. Presumably, Alfred's wall-punching tendencies had been curtailed. I ran down to Billy's room, where he was waiting with Myke, Dottie, and six rambunctious kittens. Dottie was sitting on the floor crying, and Myke was attempting to corral the kittens while Billy sat at his computer looking extremely uncomfortable.

"What's up?" I said eloquently.

"Myke wants me to take one of his cats," Billy said. "I said no, and Dottie started crying."

Dottie wiped her eyes with her sleeve and looked up at me. "I'm sorry I left you alone with my uncle," she said. "I was scared."

I couldn't blame her.

"That was really cool, you blasting through the garage door," I said.

Dottie almost smiled, then reverted to looking miserable. "He already made me forget *Charlotte's Web* once. I didn't want to forget it again, and I was afraid he'd make me forget Myke, too."

"Did your parents ask him to do it?"

She nodded and started bawling again.

Billy said, "I was just looking up some info about kids divorcing their parents."

"Seriously? You can do that?"

"It's complicated. She'd need an adult willing to adopt her, and a lawyer. I mean, it hardly ever happens."

"Even if her parents are abusing her?"

Billy shook his head. "I don't know."

"Dottie, do you have any relatives you could stay with?"

She snuffled, then said, "My grandparents on my father's side. Only they don't speak anymore."

"They can't talk?" Myke said.

"No! They can talk, but my parents won't speak to them. My dad says they're heathens because they won't go to his church. I miss them. My grandma is really nice."

I exchanged a look with Billy. "That could be good," I said.

"Only I don't know if they'd want me," she said miserably.

Bing!

"That's Alfred," Billy said, looking at his computer display. "Dottie's parents are here. They want Dottie back."

"I told my mom where we were going," Myke said, looking at Dottie. "She must have told your parents."

"That's okay," Dottie said. "They would've found me sooner or later." She took a deep breath and wiped her eyes. "I guess I've got to go."

"Maybe not," I said. "Let me and Billy handle this."

39

Fly on the Nose

Billy and I trooped upstairs, leaving Myke and Dottie in charge of the kittens. We heard Mr. and Mrs. Tisk in the foyer, arguing with Alfred.

"Master Billy does not accept unannounced visitors to his room," Alfred was explaining. "I am sure he will be with you shortly."

"I'm right here," Billy said as we entered the foyer.

"Where is my daughter?"

"Why do you ask?" I asked.

Both Tisks stabbed at me with their eyes.

"You!" said Mrs. Tisk.

"Why, yes," I agreed. "Me."

"Where is Dottie? We know she's here." He thrust a thumb at Alfred. "This clinking, clattering collection of junk has admitted as much."

"I do not clatter," Alfred said.

"Dottie is here," I admitted, "but she doesn't want to go home with you."

"That is outrageous!" Mr. Tisk exclaimed. "She is my daughter, and she will do what I say!" He shoved me aside and pushed past Billy and headed for the stairwell. Alfred, who was quicker on his motilators than I gave him credit for, quickly caught up with Mr. Tisk.

"Excuse me, sir. I detect a fly on your nose."

Fortunately for Mr. Tisk, Billy had made some adjustments to Alfred's hydraulic arms, dialing back the power to reduce the number of holes punched in the walls. Unfortunately for Mr. Tisk, he hadn't dialed it back all the way. Alfred's pneumatic arm shot out and connected solidly with Mr. Tisk's nose.

Things got very noisy and confusing after that. Mrs. Tisk became hysterical and insisted on calling an ambulance, even though Mr. Tisk's nose wasn't actually broken—it was just bleeding a little. Dottie and Myke came running upstairs to see what was going on. Dottie started screaming when she saw the blood on her father's face. Gilly arrived home right in the middle of the drama, and the kittens got out of their basket and were running all over the house. I called my parents, and they both arrived at the same time as the ambulance. Alfred made a large

pot of tea, killed an actual fly, and set about cleaning Mr. Tisk's blood out of the carpet. It was all very
confusing, but we finally got things sorted out.

Mrs. Tisk accompanied her husband to the
hospital. My mom contacted Dottie's grandparents, and they said they'd be happy to have Dottie
stay with them. My mom said she'd give Dottie a
ride, and they left together. My dad and Gilly had
to get back to the ACPOD neuroprosthetics lab to
try to reverse engineer the REMEMBER machine.
Mr. Rausch would not be much help, according to
Gilly. He had loaded the entirety of *Wikipedia* into
his brain.

"All of it?" I said.

"So it seems," said Gilly. "All eight hundred
million pages."

"That's a lot."

"Yes. It didn't leave room for anything else.
And he did it without an animal to store his deleted
memories. I'm afraid Ernest Rausch doesn't even
remember his own name. He'll probably have to be
toilet trained all over again."

Myke had captured all the kittens and had
them back in their basket. "I'm going to take these
back to Clawz-n-Pawz," he said. "Let me know if
you change your mind, Billy. This little orange one
likes you."

After Myke left, it was just me, Billy, and Alfred.

"That was a pretty good punch, Alfred," I said.

"I am programmed to eliminate many varieties of invasive species," Alfred said.

"Anyway, good job."

"Thank you."

Billy and I watched him roll off on his motilators.

"I think we're going to have to do some more tweaking," Billy said.

"I kind of like him the way he is."

Billy laughed, then said, "By the way, I got a hit on your e-book hacker."

I had almost forgotten about that. "Was it the Tisks?"

"Nope."

I waited for more.

"You're not even going to believe this," Billy said.

40

The Hacker

"You again," said Ms. Pfleuger.

I was standing in front of her desk with my arms crossed, looking up at her.

"It was you," I said.

She tipped her head quizzically. "Me?"

"You hacked the e-books." I looked to make sure Billy was still with me. He was, but he was standing back a ways, looking rather nervous.

"Oh. That." She laughed. "My little demonstration."

"Demonstration!" I said.

"Yes. In every sense of the word. I hope that you will take the lesson to heart."

I stared at her in disbelief. *"Lesson?"*

"Yes. Storing information digitally is dangerous and unreliable. Books, on the other hand"—she gestured at the thousands of books surrounding us—"are solid, real, and dependable."

"What if your library catches on fire?" Billy asked.

"If these books are destroyed, there are still thousands of other copies in other libraries all over the world. But if an e-book is damaged, every other copy of that e-book might suffer the same fate, as you have seen." She looked at me. "What did you do when your digital copy of *Charlotte's Web* was altered?"

"I looked for the paper-book version," I admitted.

"Exactly."

"But you broke the law," I said. "And what about all the kids who are trying to read *Charlotte's Web* on their tabs?"

"I feel bad about that." Ms. Pfleuger looked slightly chastened. "But you can't make an omelet without breaking a few eggs."

"It's got nothing to do with omelets!"

"True," she said, looking down at her lap.

"And kids are not eggs. You're supposed to be a librarian."

"I *am* a librarian!" she said, her face slowly reddening.

I was too mad to be scared, so I just kept on going. "Every kid who tried to read Charlotte over the last few days thinks it's a really awful book that doesn't make any sense at all."

"It was just for a few days," she said in a small voice. Her eyes looked funny, or at least what I could see of them through those thick glasses. "I changed it back this morning." Her voice sounded funny too. She held up the laptop on her desk and turned the screen toward us. "See? *Charlotte's Web* has been restored to its original version."

A tear dribbled down her cheek. The Pformidable Pfleuger was crying.

Suddenly all the anger drained out of me.

"But *why*?" I asked.

She pushed up her glasses and wiped her eyes with the back of her hand, looking anything but pformidable. "It was not my finest moment," she said.

"How?" Billy asked. "That was a first-class worm you set loose. How did you know how to do that?"

"It was a simple hack, really." Ms. Pfleuger took out a paisley handkerchief and blew her nose. "I haven't always been a librarian, you know. Up until ten years ago I worked for your father as a software engineer. But then I decided to follow my dream of being a librarian. I just really love books."

"E-books are books too," I said.

"I know that." She sighed. "But I worry that people will forget paper books the same way we've forgotten scrolls and stone tablets. I wrote that virus a few months ago, just to see if it could be done. I didn't plan to use it, but then that awful man Mr. Tisk showed up, and . . . I was afraid he'd convince the town council that my library was irrelevant. We've been having money problems, you see. The council is already cutting back our funding. They say that Flinkwater County Library—with all their computers—better meets the needs of the people. Flinkwater Memorial could be shut down.

"So I set the virus loose. Just for one book, *Charlotte's Web*. Just to show people how important it is to have *real* books. I always intended to change it back." She blew her nose again. "I see now that maybe it wasn't such a good idea."

"I don't see why we can't have both paper books and e-books," I said.

"Perhaps you are right. I don't suppose e-books will be going away."

Billy said, "You know, I still remember coming here when I was a little kid. You used to have Saturday story time, remember?"

Ms. Pfleuger nodded. "A lot of kids came here back then." She looked at me and frowned. "Some of them chewed gum, as I recall."

"I really liked story time," Billy said.

"Me too," I agreed.

"I stopped doing that when the groups got smaller and smaller, and one Saturday nobody showed up."

"You should start it up again. I bet my cousin Kellan would come. He's three. And I know he's got lots of friends from preschool."

Ms. Pfleuger smiled sadly. "That would be nice, but I'm afraid I won't be working here for long." Her shoulders slumped. "I'll lose the library for sure now."

"Maybe not." I looked at Billy, and I could tell we were both thinking the same thing. "Everybody makes a mistake now and then, right?"

41

Tuna Fish

When I got home, Dad was in the kitchen eating a sandwich. Barney and Mr. Peebles were both there, looking lovingly up at him. Or maybe they were looking at his sandwich.

"Dad," I said, "we have to save the library."

He said, "The library needs saving?"

"Yes! Ms. Pfleuger says the city council is going to take away their funding."

"I thought you weren't a big fan of paper books." He took a big bite of his sandwich.

"I'm not, but . . . Is that tuna fish?"

He nodded, chewing.

"I thought you didn't like fish," I said.

"I don't," he said. "But for some reason I had a yen for tuna. By the way, I have good news. Gilly figured out how the REMEMBER machine works. I got my missing memories back. I remember

Barney now. It turned out to be quite simple. The animals where our memories were stored have wireless transmitters implanted in their cerebellums. All that's necessary to reverse the process is to put that headset on and let the machine run for a few minutes with the animal nearby. The tricky part was matching up the right animal with the right person. We were able to unscramble enough of Rausch's notes to do that. Billy's memories are stored in that bulldog, as you know. Next time you see him, he should be back to the old Billy."

"What animal were your memories in?"

"Mr. Peebles here."

"Mrowp," said Mr. Peebles.

"Maybe that's why you're eating tuna fish," I said. "Some of his cat memories might have leaked into your brain."

He looked at the sandwich in his hand and set it down. "That had not occurred to me."

"It might also explain why Mr. Peebles risked his life to save me. Because part of *you* was inside *him*."

He regarded Mr. Peebles thoughtfully, then tore the remains of his sandwich in half and gave it to the cats. "That might also explain some other odd thoughts I've been having. I keep seeing the words 'some pig.'"

"Dad, that's from *Charlotte's Web!*"

"Really? I'd love to read that book!"

"I gave it back to Dottie Tisk. It's her favorite book ever."

"Interesting. Dottie's missing memories were also stored in Mr. Peebles. There must have been some leakage."

"Dad! Gross!" I was horrified. It's one thing to have a father who is part cat, but a dad who is part teenage girl . . . that was too much.

"Speaking of cats, your friend Myke Duchakis just stopped by with a basket full of kittens," he said. "I told him we had all the cats we could handle. He's a very nice young man. Quite handsome, don't you think? Ginger? Are you okay?"

"Sorry. I just threw up a little in my mouth." I didn't tell him that Dottie had a crush on Myke. It would only confuse him more.

"You should go rinse it out," he suggested.

"Good idea." As I left the room I heard somebody—I couldn't tell whether it was Mr. Peebles or my dad—say, "Meow."

Okay, kind of weird having a dad who was part cat and part Dottie Tisk, but even worse would be having a fiancé who was part bulldog. I grabbed my dad's WheelBot and took off for the neuro-prosthetics lab.

I was too late. I arrived at the lab just as they

were disconnecting Billy from the Rauschinator. Gertrude was on the floor next to him licking her butt.

"Billy?" I said.

Billy looked at me. His eyes lit up and he smiled.

"Ginger!" He got out of the chair and came toward me and wrapped his arms around me, and he—

—licked my face.

42

Leakage

"Eww!" I pushed him away.

"What?" he said with a hurt, hangdog expression.

"You just licked me!"

"I did?" He looked confused. "I'm just glad to see you. Again. I mean, I remember everything now."

"Great, but I think maybe you remember some stuff you shouldn't."

Gilly was watching us and smiling.

"It's not funny!" I said.

"Actually, it is," Gilly said.

"What if he tries to lick his own butt?"

"Don't worry—it won't last. A certain amount of memory leakage is unavoidable, but a few days from now Billy's memories will settle back into their old neural pathways. The remnants of Gertrude's memory will fade away."

"I hope so," I said. "Having my face licked once is quite enough."

Billy said, "You don't mind when Gertrude licks you."

"*Gertrude* is a *dog!*"

"Okay, no more licking. I also promise not to chase balls or chew on bones. At least not when you're around."

As I have mentioned before, I can be somewhat sarcastic at times, but I do not like it when other people are sarcastic with me. I gave him the evil eye, but he was grinning.

"It's really nice to have you back in my head," he said.

"It's nice to be there," I said, which made no sense at all, since I myself had never visited the inside of his head. But he knew what I meant, and that was what was important. I think if Gilly hadn't been sitting right there we would have had a nice boy-girl-style kiss.

"I have some more good news," Billy said. "The library is saved!"

"I've agreed to make a substantial contribution to that dusty old museum," Gilly said. "Despite the fact that Olivia Pfleuger, who used to be one of my best programmers, quit ACPOD to bury herself in dead trees." He was trying to sound grumpy, but he couldn't help smiling. "After all, we can't have one of the smartest software engineers on the planet out there vandalizing our literature, right?"

"So she's not going to jail or anything?" I said.

"Certainly not. But I will require her to make sure every person who attempted to read the corrupted version of *Charlotte's Web* is notified, apologized to, and offered a free paper copy of the book."

"That sounds really complicated. How can she track down all those people?"

"Olivia may be a fool, but she also happens to be a genius. I'm sure she'll figure out how to do it."

All that happened a few weeks ago. Since then, Ms. Pfleuger has added two computers to her library and restarted her Saturday morning story-time program. Last week twenty preschoolers and kindergarteners came to hear her read *Where the Wild Things Are*. I was there too, volunteering to help with kid control. Those four-year-olds are monsters!

Dottie Tisk is living with her grandparents now, and she's back at school. Last week I saw her wearing one of Myke Duchakis's ANIMALS ARE PEOPLE TOO T-shirts. Billy was right. A girl who would crash through a closed garage door on an ATV was a lot tougher than she appeared.

Ernest Rausch never did remember who he was or what he had done, but he seemed to know pretty much everything else. He had not only downloaded *Wikipedia*, but all 400,000 words in the *Oxford English Dictionary*. He immediately began sharing information with anyone who would listen. Do you want to know how fast an aardvark can run? Rausch is your go-to guy. Questions about the royal family of nineteenth century Portugal? Ask Rausch.

"He'll probably have to be institutionalized," Dad told me. "The man knows everything, but he can barely feed himself. Knowing a lot is not the same as being smart."

"He's still going to jail, right?"

"There's no point in bringing him to trial. He remembers nothing of what he did. In a sense, he is not Ernest Rausch anymore. He's a completely different person."

"I guess that's a good thing. I didn't much care for the original."

Billy is back to normal, almost. He does bark now and then, but I think he does it just to bug me. I try to ignore it. Gilly, whose missing memories were divided between the goat and Gertrude, occasionally lets out a random bleat. Dad no longer eats tuna fish, but he does curl up on the sofa and purr sometimes.

Fortunately, this is Flinkwater, where eccentric behaviors are considered normal.

Speaking of Flinkwater, I got an incomplete on my report for Mr. Westerburg because, well, I didn't complete it. But I did solve the mystery eventually. Just last week, as a matter of fact.

43

Walter Funk

I'm still a big fan of e-books, but after the Pformidable Pfleuger's vandalism I'd been thinking more about how easy it would be to alter any digital file. Every time I read an e-book I had to check it against a paper copy, because people could be out there vandalizing e-books all the time and I'd never know it.

I had just read the entire *Lord of the Rings* trilogy and loved it, but it was so different from the movies that it made me wonder if it had been hacked, so I went downstairs to see if my dad had a paper copy.

I checked his shelves from top to bottom. No *Lord of the Rings*, but there were a lot of really strange books that used to belong to his grandfather—things that aren't even available as e-books. I was looking at a book from 1911 called *Tom Swift and His Electric Rifle* when a framed black-and-white photograph on the wall between the bookshelves caught my eye. Dad had lots of old photos on his wall. I had never paid much attention to them, but this one was a picture of a sign with letters made out of painted wooden slats. The sign read:

Flinkwater? The picture looked really old—older even than the book I was holding. I noticed a barely legible note scrawled in the margin: *Uncle Walt's Farm, 1886.*

1886. That was a year before the founding of Flinkwater. So why did the sign say Flinkwater when Flinkwater didn't even exist yet? And who was Uncle Walt?

I stared at that photo for a long time. Did it really say FLINKWATER? It looked like two words, "FLINK" and "WATER." And there was too much space between the *A* and the *T* in "WATER." And the bottom of the *L* in "FLINK" looked like it had been broken off. I stared and stared, and all of a sudden it hit me.

"*Daaaaad!*" I yelled in my *Help-I'm-being-
eaten-by-zombies* voice.

It took him forever to get there—if there'd been
actual zombies, I'd be lunch.

"What is it?" he said, completely unsurprised by
the absence of walking dead.

I pointed a shaking finger at the photo.

"What. Is. That?" I inquired.

"That. Is. A. Photograph," he replied.

"Of what?"

He squinted at the picture.

"I found that in your mother's collection. It
looks like an old sign."

"No duh! But what *is* it?"

"I suppose it's a sign at the edge of town from
way back when."

"Who is Uncle Walt?"

He shrugged. "I have no idea."

"*Mooooom!*" I yelled. Dad clapped his hands
over his ears and backed out of the room. A minute
later my mother peeked in through the doorway.

"Are you all right?"

"No! Who is Uncle Walt and what is this picture?"

She examined the photo and read the inscrip-
tion.

"Walter Funk was your great-great-great-
granduncle," she said. "He settled here back in the
1870s."

"Before Flinkwater was Flinkwater."

"Yes." She smiled. "How is your research going?"

"Very well, no thanks to you! Do you know how many hours I spent trying to figure out why Flinkwater is called Flinkwater?"

"And now you know. That sign" — she pointed at the photo — "probably originally read 'FUNK, WALTER.'"

"I sort of figured that out," I said.

"Part of the *U* broke off, the comma fell off, and the *L* in Walter disappeared. When new settlers arrived and incorporated the town, they saw Uncle Walt's old sign and assumed it said 'Flinkwater,' so that's what they named the town."

"You let me do all that research when you knew the answer all along?"

"Yes," she said. "Because I knew you could do it."

The funny thing was, I wasn't even mad. It was actually kind of cool that Flinkwater, Iowa, was named after my family, and Mom and I were the only ones who knew it. We were the Keepers of the Secret of Flinkwater.

"I guess it's better than if they named the town Funk," I said.

"That's right, and don't you ever forget it."

"I won't," I said. "I never forget anything."

Present or Future?

Ginger Crump and her friends live in the future. How far in the future? Who knows? More than a year, but less than fifty years. Ginger's world is not all that different from ours. People in Flinkwater use cell phones; they text; they use the Internet. But they have a few things we don't have: robot butlers, antigravity drones, and guns that fire invisible stun rays. How much of Ginger's world will become a reality in the near future? How much is real already?

Chapter 1 • DustBots

DustBots are small machines that scurry around the house picking up all sorts of dust and dirt. In Flinkwater, just about every home has several of them. Today, we have Roombas, Neatos, and several other brands of automatic vacuum cleaners—sort of like big, clunky versions of the DustBot, but they don't empty themselves, and they aren't nearly as cute! *Future! Soon!*

Chapter 3 • *E-books*

Everybody knows about e-books—you might be reading this on one right now! But most books today are paper books made out of dead trees. Will e-books ever completely replace paper books the way paper books replaced papyrus scrolls and stone tablets? Maybe, but not for a while. *Present!*

Chapter 4 • *Alfred*

Alfred, the Bateses' robot butler, reminds me of the robot from the 1960s TV series *Lost in Space*. We do have human-size robots that can perform various tasks, but compared to Alfred, they are very limited. We might have robot butlers some day, but not for many, many years. *Future!*

Chapter 13 • *Antigravity drones*

Everybody knows drones are real. The military has been using them for years, and you can buy a propeller-driven drone at your local toy store right now. But Gilly's AG-3601 drone uses antigravity instead of propellers.

Today we have maglev trains that allow heavy trains to glide over miles of track without touching the rails. They use electromagnetic force to lift the train, but they do not actually cancel the force of gravity. Simple propellers are similar—they counter gravity by pushing air down. But the antigravity powering Gilly's drone is a more advanced technology, and one we do not yet have. *Future!*

Chapter 19 • *WheelBots*

Gyroscopically controlled unicycles are available right now! They might not be as fast as Billy's WheelBot, but they're still pretty cool. *Present!*

Chapter 26 • *The REMEMBER machine*

Is it possible to insert information into the human brain? In a way, that's what reading does! But downloading complex information from a computer directly to the brain is not yet possible, and even if we figure out how to do it, it might not be all that useful. For example, if you could download this whole book into your head in a few seconds, you would lose the experience of reading the story, and what fun would that be? *Future (maybe)!*

Chapter 26 • *Memory overload*

When you learn something, do you have to forget something else to make room in your brain? Maybe. The human brain has been estimated to have a capacity of between ten and one hundred terabytes. Today, *Wikipedia* contains around ten terabytes of information, and it gets bigger every day. So if you could download all of *Wikipedia* into your brain, would your head explode, or would some of the information already there get pushed out? I used to know the answer, but I forgot! *Future (maybe)!*

Chapter 40 • *Bookless libraries*

Today, computers have become a big part of the services offered by most libraries—and there are a few libraries that have no paper books at all. *Present.* Will bookless libraries become the norm in the future? *Who knows?*

Chapter 40 • *Hacking Charlotte's Web*

Could a book really be altered on every server and every reading device in the world? Maybe not today, but as our devices become more and more connected, it is conceivable. Paper books matter! *Future!*

31901060400548